WARRIOR OF LIGHT

The mirror broke in pieces~~~~~~~~~and damp,
the mist of ages, locked deep in a cave for centuries,
poured out. With it, a figure fell towards them—a
man with tousled hair and a streaked, matted beard.
The stench in the room was of old bones and
battles and armour.

Ralph and Maddy stared. The man lying on the
floor was certainly not Uncle Alistair. There was only
one person it could be . . .

An ancient legend comes to life as the figures of
four horsemen emerge from an age-old painting on
the schoolhouse wall. Aelfric is summoned from his
long sleep in the cave of black stars. Ralph and Maddy,
visiting Uncle Alistair, are caught up once again in the
war between Light and Darkness, time and the End of
Everything.

WILLIAM RAEPER was born in Kirkcaldy,
Scotland in 1959. He wrote many books, including
a biography of the great Scottish story-teller,
George MacDonald. He lived in Scotland, Paris,
Oxford, Norway and Nepal.

In 1992 he was flying to Nepal when the plane
crashed into the Himalayan mountains. William is
remembered especially for his laughter and his
friendship.

Warrior of Light is the sequel to *A Witch in Time* and
was finished a few weeks before he died.

FOR TESS IONA
THANK YOU FOR MAKING ME
AN UNCLE

WARRIOR
OF LIGHT

WILLIAM RAEPER

A LION PAPERBACK
Oxford · Batavia · Sydney

Copyright © 1993 the estate of William Raeper

The author asserts the moral right
to be identified as the author of this work

Published by
Lion Publishing plc
Sandy Lane West, Oxford, England
ISBN 0 7459 2509 X
Albatross Books Pty Ltd
PO Box 320, Sutherland, NSW 2232, Australia
ISBN 0 7324 0673 0

First edition 1993

A catalogue record for this book is available
from the British Library

Printed and bound in Great Britain
by Cox & Wyman Ltd, Reading

'The light shines in the darkness, but the darkness has not overcome it.'

The Gospel of John, chapter 1, verse 5

1

The train shot into the tunnel so suddenly that Ralph almost jumped out of his seat.

'How long now?' asked Maddy. She was sitting with her tired head pressed against the window.

'I don't know,' Ralph shrugged dismissively. 'It's a long time since I've been, and we went by car last time.'

Ralph looked out of the window. Dazzling, fresh sunlight now flooded the dusty train compartment. Outside, the country was criss-crossed with ripening fields which fell away into the distant, shimmering haze.

'There'——the word echoed in Ralph's head. He had hardly ever been 'there' before—only once or twice when he was very young. He recalled the smell of polish in the hall of Uncle Alistair's house and the solid, forbidding wooden furniture which he had not been allowed to touch. And now he and Maddy were going to stay 'there'.

Ralph's Uncle Alistair came and went without warning. 'A law unto himself,' Ralph's mother would mutter. But Uncle Alistair was not a law unto himself, as Ralph had slowly begun to understand. He was a law unto something else, something deeper.

Postcards would arrive at odd times—from South America, from the South Pacific, even from Tibet. Ralph's mother would examine them, read them out loud and stick them to the white tiles above the kitchen sink. 'Oh, that brother of mine,' she would sigh.

Ralph's mother thought Uncle Alistair should stay at

home, not go hopping off to places where he might catch something nasty, or even disappear. But Ralph felt certain that even if his uncle did suddenly disappear, he would appear again, somehow, one day. It *was* odd. When Uncle Alistair looked at you he gave you the feeling that he was in touch with things which were out of reach for most ordinary people.

A year ago last Easter he had come to stay while Ralph's parents were away. What happened then* only served to confirm what Ralph had always felt about his uncle. There was something strange, something mysterious, about him. Wherever he went, it seemed, extraordinary things happened. It was during Uncle Alistair's visit to Ralph that he and Maddy had become such good friends. Now they were going to stay with him. What would happen? What could happen? Ralph wasn't sure he even wanted to think about it—because he knew that with Uncle Alistair *anything* could happen.

Maddy shifted in her seat and pressed her fists under her chin. The arrival of the strange man sitting opposite them had put an end to their conversation. They both felt uncomfortable. Maddy nudged Ralph and he darted a glance at the worried-looking man.

Ralph had found it hard to take his eyes off the stranger since he had boarded the train at Reading. Ralph and Maddy had had to change trains there, with an hour to wait for their next train. When it came in they walked through a couple of carriages until they came to an empty compartment. It was First Class, but there was a peeling sticker glued to the window which stated FOR USE OF PASSENGERS TRAVELLING STANDARD CLASS.

'Great,' said Maddy, 'we can be more private here.' She bounced down next to the window and watched as Ralph

* You can read this story in *A Witch in Time*

put up the bags. The train started with a jolt. That was when the man arrived, squeezing his fat bulk down the corridor.

The man was dressed in a grey-belted coat that seemed all wrong for summer. His head was bald and shiny at the front and he was sweating when he entered the compartment. That was the first thing Ralph noticed. The man sat down nervously on the edge of his seat. Every so often he took another piece of screwed-up tissue out of his coat pocket and wiped his glistening forehead. His breathing was heavy, with an unhealthy-sounding wheeze. It seemed to fill the compartment.

Maddy and Ralph sat in tense silence, unable to speak. They had been looking forward to the rail journey and now they felt cheated.

Unlike most grown-ups on trains, this man did not pull out a newspaper or a book and begin to read. Instead, he just sat with his eyes closed, cradling his suitcase in both arms and wiping his dripping forehead. His clothes smelled strongly of pipe tobacco, mixed with something else which neither Ralph nor Maddy recognized. His coat-flaps were drawn round the suitcase so that no one passing could see what he was holding. Every movement of the train made him open his eyes and start with anxiety, clutching the suitcase even tighter.

Ralph and Maddy could see the case fairly clearly. It was brown, scuffed and frayed at the edges and had silver locks. It couldn't have been too heavy or the man wouldn't have been able to hold it like that.

'I wonder what's in it,' Maddy mouthed, turning her head so that the man could not possibly see. Ralph shook his head.

After a few stops the ticket man slid open the door.

'Your tickets, please!'

The man with the suitcase opened his eyes. He scrabbled in his pockets and eventually pulled out a sorry-looking ticket. Ralph and Maddy handed theirs over.

'Everything all right?'

'Yes, thank you,' Maddy said. 'But is it Lower Chernton next stop?'

'After Howsworth,' replied the ticket man. 'Ten or fifteen minutes to Howsworth and another quarter of an hour to Lower Chernton. You should be there in half an hour. We're running a bit slow today.'

At the mention of Lower Chernton the man with the suitcase shivered. He started to search his pockets again, this time for a tissue.

'Oh, dear!' he murmured, rubbing his eyes. 'Oh, dear, dear!'

The ticket man, not knowing what to make of this, shook his head and ducked out of the compartment. Ralph decided that he had to say *something* to break the silence.

'Do you think I should get the bags down?' he said to Maddy. 'I'm thirsty.'

'Yes, if you like,' Maddy answered. 'Is Uncle Alistair coming to meet us?' Her mind was clearly on other things.

'Oh, he'll be there,' said Ralph confidently.

As Ralph stood up to reach for the bags he noticed something unnerving. He couldn't tell Maddy about it— anyway, he wasn't completely sure. There was a mirror above the seat, and a flash of sunlight drew Ralph's eyes towards it. He could see the suitcase reflected in the mirror. *But the strange man had no reflection at all!*

Ralph stared hard at the mirror, then looked at the man again. He was sure now. When he looked into the glass the man wasn't there. All of a sudden Ralph felt a stab of fear. But he made himself act normally and haul the bags down. He didn't want the man to become ... suspicious. 'Suspicious'—a strange word to come into his head—

especially on an ordinary rail journey.

Ralph placed the two bags beside him on the seat. 'We may as well have the orange juice now,' he said.

'OK,' said Maddy.

Ralph was still wondering about the mirror. Had the glare of bright sunlight simply confused him? He looked at the man again—and saw that his face was frozen in terror. He had shrunk back into his coat and his fat, flabby face was devoid of colour. This time Maddy, too, noticed that something was wrong.

Moving steadily down the narrow corridor outside their compartment was a passenger dressed in a white shirt, black trousers and wearing dark sunglasses. This man was slim, almost too thin, and there was something easy and cat-like in the way he carried himself. His gaze swivelled to left and right as he advanced. He seemed to be looking for something—or someone.

On the corridor side of the compartment was a faded blue curtain, screening passengers from the prying eyes of passers-by. The man with the suitcase pressed himself back behind this, against his headrest, scarcely breathing. When at last the man in dark glasses had moved further up the train, the man with the suitcase stood up. He dumped the case on the blue tartan seat.

'I can't . . . I just can't go through . . .' he muttered in panic. Then, pulling himself together and seeming to make some kind of decision, he turned to Ralph and Maddy. 'You two,' he said, 'will you look after this suitcase for me? A boy and a girl—yes, that's the only way.'

Not waiting for an answer, he turned and stumbled out of the compartment.

'Well, there's definitely something funny about *him*,' said Maddy.

' . . . like he's worried?'

11

'You can say that again. He seemed really frightened. He was sweating so much, I thought he was going to melt!'

Houses and fences passed by outside as the train slowed for Howsworth. The village station was neat and well cared for. Bright flowers spelled HOWSWORTH in coloured letters all along the bank by the track. A few passengers got off with their bags, and one or two others got on. It was still too early for people to be travelling home from work.

'Look!' exclaimed Maddy. She stabbed her finger against the smeared window.

'What is it?' asked Ralph.

The coat was unmistakable. Ralph saw it slip in and out among the passengers on the platform. Coat-tails flapping, the man waddled up the station steps, looking from the back like a badger.

'Why on earth has he gone?' asked Maddy. 'Isn't it ...'

' ... strange.' Ralph finished her sentence. He began to chew the ends of his fingers.

'He's running away. And he's left his precious suitcase with us!'

The suitcase lay exposed on the soft, dusty seat, looking battered and lost.

'It's not heavy,' said Ralph. He reached over and picked it up. 'I guessed that from the way he was holding it. It feels as though there's nothing in it.'

There was nothing on it either, Ralph noticed—except a double-snake insignia fashioned in flaking gold leaf. The two snakes wound round one another in a perfect circle, with their tails tucked into their mouths.

'It looks a bit ...' Ralph began.

' ... creepy,' said Maddy. 'What are we going to do?'

'Show it to Uncle Alistair and hand it in, I suppose.'

'But Ralph, the man gave it to *us*!'

The train jolted and started again. Ralph yawned. 'Next stop Lower Chernton.'

Uncle Alistair was on the platform to meet them. As the train drew into the station, they could see his head above all the rest. He threw his arms wide when he saw them.

'At last,' he smiled. 'And only ten minutes late! Lovely to see you both. You must tell me what you've been up to. I expect you're hungry. I wasn't altogether sure what you liked eating, so I bought just about everything!'

Uncle Alistair waved one of his slender hands in the air and laughed. How tall he was, taller even than Ralph remembered.

'I've not been back very long,' he said. 'But you know that. Business in India. So the house isn't looking its best. Still, I always say that after the first three years the windows can't get any dirtier! And Gail from the village comes in and tidies up twice a week. Your mother wouldn't approve, Ralph. She's been trying to lick me into shape for years. But what's this?'

Uncle Alistair's eyes were fixed on the suitcase.

'Er ... a suitcase,' said Ralph.

'I can see that! But it's not yours, is it? It's more the kind of thing Granny uses.'

'Yes ...' Ralph hadn't thought of it like that.

'A man left it on the train,' said Maddy.

'So we thought we should hand it in,' said Ralph.

'Good thinking.' Uncle Alistair frowned. 'This man ... Got off the train, did he, and left his suitcase. Just like that?'

'Not exactly,' said Maddy quietly.

'Pretty careless! With all these announcements about taking your luggage with you, you'd have thought ... But maybe he did think, whoever he was. Sorry, Maddy, what did you say?'

'I said "Not exactly." The man in our compartment sort of gave it to us. Or left it with us, anyway.'

Uncle Alistair crouched down to look closer. His wiry figure shadowed the suitcase.

'Well, well,' he murmured as he fingered the gold snakes. 'How curious that they should turn up here.'

'The snakes?' said Maddy. 'Do you know about them?'

'A bit. You see, Maddy, the form of these snakes is very old. Snakes can mean many different things—power, healing, wisdom, evil, mystery...'

'... and magic?' suggested Ralph, in a half-afraid voice.

'That too, unfortunately,' Uncle Alistair replied.

'So are we going to hand the case in?'

'Oh, I should think...' Uncle Alistair rose, smoothed his trousers and swung round. He was about to finish his sentence when something he saw cut him short. The passengers who had got out of the train were still showing their tickets at the exit. The man with dark glasses was last in line behind a woman and a toddler. He had put on a black jacket.

As they watched, another man in similar clothes went to meet him. They might have been twins. The two men shook hands, then suddenly broke into an explosive argument. Ralph and Maddy and Uncle Alistair watched in fascination, though they could not hear what the two men were saying. The man from the train extended his hands as if in apology. The man who had come to meet him shook his head in disgust and stalked away. The first man hesitated a moment, staring hard at the place on the platform where Ralph, Maddy and Uncle Alistair were standing.

'A boy and a girl,' breathed Maddy to herself, echoing the fat man's words.

Uncle Alistair had dropped the jacket he was carrying over the suitcase so that it was hidden from view. The man took a last, lingering look at them and walked out to the car park.

'So, are we going to hand the case in?' asked Ralph.

Uncle Alistair seemed to have changed his mind. He was doubtful now. 'It's very light,' he remarked as he picked it up.

'I know,' said Ralph.

'Why *not* hand it in?' asked Maddy.

'You said he gave it to you, didn't you?'

'Yes.' Maddy and Ralph nodded uncomfortably.

'Then you might say it's come to us for... uh... safekeeping. There might be good reason, you know. Maybe the case needs to be safe. Maybe it wouldn't be safe if I handed it in to Lost Property. Anyway, it seems to me more like Found Property than Lost Property. I think we should take it home for now. We'll have a look at it and if it's all right I'll drop it off at the station later this evening. No one will mind that.'

'What do you mean, if it's "all right"?' questioned Maddy.

'Let's just get into the car, Maddy,' urged Uncle Alistair, 'you ought to know by now that you can't always explain everything at the beginning.'

It was just a short distance to Uncle Alistair's. They drove up the High Street past all the shops and then turned right, down a lane. Uncle Alistair's house was set back, slightly hidden from the road. All you could see above the surrounding trees were a few reddish chimney-pots. The house itself lay behind a gate, up a short, mossy drive. It was red brick with white-painted window frames. There was not much garden at the back of the house, but at the front the lawn was wide and well-trimmed and gently sloping until it met the tall, rough grass by the river.

The car followed the drive round to the front of the house. Uncle Alistair switched off the engine and

Maddy and Ralph rushed up the steps to the front door. From the top they could see the river, a flowing silver ribbon dotted with brown rocks. Opposite, fenced off, was a thick wood; and then, on either side of the wood, grassy fields.

'It's quiet here,' remarked Maddy.

'Usually,' said Uncle Alistair, glancing down rather worriedly at the case.

He took out his key and opened the front door. The hall smelled of polish, just as Ralph remembered, and sunlight splashed over the uneven floor tiles from a skylight above. The hall led through to the kitchen with doors off to the living-room and Uncle Alistair's study. A bundle of coats and jackets hung on hooks near the door. Framed pictures and old prints hung on the walls. There were two bookcases crammed with books in the hall and on either side of the phone a row of trailing plants.

'So here we are! I'll put the kettle on—that's for me. But what would you like? Juice? Cake? Biscuits?'

'I'd like to look inside the suitcase,' said Ralph with determination.

'Right away? Before anything else? Are you sure?' Uncle Alistair stopped.

'Yes, right away!' Ralph was sure.

'OK, then,' Uncle Alistair conceded. 'Let's go into the living-room.'

Uncle Alistair's living-room, at the front of the house, had a large bay window overlooking the river. The brownish carpet was thick and springy. Chinese rugs hugged the grate and a huge mirror with gilt edges graced the fireplace. The sofa, scattered with patterned cushions from India, was drawn up to face the television. There were one or two old pictures of relatives on the wall, but the largest picture was of ancient ruins in Rome.

In front of the sofa was a table piled with books and

newspapers. Uncle Alistair set the suitcase carefully on top. The double snakes gleamed up at him in the glare of the sun. It was five o'clock now—the long day was drawing to a close. School had broken up two weeks ago. It was the peaceful height of summer.

'Is the suitcase locked?' asked Maddy, peering close.

'No, it's not locked. Look. So no one's trying to keep us out. Oh, dear, I'd much rather not get mixed up in all this! But I suppose we must, since the suitcase was given to you. Are you ready?'

'Yes,' nodded Ralph, wondering what his uncle thought they were getting mixed up in.

Uncle Alistair took a deep breath and clicked open the silver locks. It was easily done. Two sharp movements with his thumbs and the fasteners sprang open.

'I really don't know *what* will be inside,' he said anxiously. With extreme caution he lifted the lid.

'Well!' he said.

Maddy gasped and turned to Ralph. Ralph simply stared. For a moment all they could hear was the ticking of the carriage clock on the mantelpiece. Nothing moved except for the pattern of sunlight on the carpet.

'So now we know,' said Uncle Alistair.

Ralph gaped into the case over his uncle's extended arms. Inside the suitcase was nothing, nothing at all. That is not to say that the suitcase was empty—simply, there was Nothing in it.

The suitcase appeared to have no bottom—just empty blackness without a glimmer of light, stretching down, down to infinity.

'Careful, Ralph,' warned Uncle Alistair, but the warning came too late.

Ralph slipped his arm into the case—and it disappeared up to the elbow.

'But that's impossible!' gasped Maddy.

'Indeed it is,' said Uncle Alistair grimly.

'It's not hot or cold or anything,' said Ralph. 'I can't *feel* anything at all. It's just . . . nothing . . .' He drew out his arm and looked at it. 'No harm done.'

Maddy stared into the emptiness of the case for a moment, hypnotized by it. 'Is it bad? Is it good?' she asked. 'What is it?'

'It's . . . Nothing,' said Uncle Alistair. 'Can't you see that? Not bad, not good. And I don't trust things that seem to be one thing and turn out to be something quite different. Things should be what they are.'

'So what is this?' asked Ralph. All of a sudden he felt helpless.

'Your guess is as good as mine,' said Uncle Alistair. 'But one thing is certain—I'll not be taking this suitcase back to the station this evening. We must hang on to it for a while longer!'

2

Supper that evening was a subdued meal.

Uncle Alistair had shut the suitcase immediately and stowed it between the fireplace and the television. Ralph could not stop thinking about it. He and Maddy unpacked, then went downstairs to find Uncle Alistair in the kitchen.

'That suitcase...' began Ralph. 'There's something creepy about it.'

'Yes, there is.' Uncle Alistair's voice came through a cloud of steam. He was arranging pots of potatoes and peas on the cooker in the kitchen. A steak pie was warming in the oven.

The steamed-up kitchen windows overlooked the small garden at the back of the house, with its patch of lawn. The kitchen had a long, scrubbed wooden table with four chairs round it. Papers, keys, a burst bag of oranges, money and bills lay spread all over it.

'You can set the table, Ralph. The stuff you need's in that drawer over there.'

Ralph cleared and laid the table, and they sat down to eat.

'We should go down to the river before it gets dark,' said Uncle Alistair. He sliced the pie into even portions. 'It's lovely in the evening.'

'But what about the suitcase?' asked Maddy. 'What are we going to do with it now?'

'We are going to wait,' Uncle Alistair responded.

'Why?' said Ralph. 'What has it got to do with us,

anyway? Can't we just get rid of it?'

'Well,'—Uncle Alistair sat down with a flourish—'if it really has nothing to do with us, nothing will happen, will it? If, on the other hand, we *are* involved in some way, as your friend on the train suggested, then we are caught up in it, whether we like it or not.'

'I don't follow,' said Maddy. She crumbled the pastry crust with her fork.

'The point is, we can't simply dodge things,' Uncle Alistair answered. 'We have to do what needs to be done. Maybe we can see things other people can't.'

He stuck out his elbows and began to eat, blowing loudly on a chunk of potato to cool it. 'There is some great power within that case, that's clear. What it is, exactly, or how it got there, I don't know. But it seems to me that the case could be a way into something, like a kind of tunnel. Now, if the case *is* a tunnel, someone will want to go through it. But why—and where to? What could lie at the other end?'

Uncle Alistair waved his fork in small, neat circles as he talked. 'If I just take the case back to the station and forget about it, whoever it was made your friend on the train so scared will probably turn up and claim it. And if something dangerous *is* going on, that won't do at all. I knew there was *something* peculiar about that case the moment I saw the snakes. It seems to me that it would be irresponsible to let it go.'

'But if they, whoever "they" are, find out that we have the case . . .' began Ralph.

' . . . then we'll find out who "they" are sooner rather than later, and the sooner the better, I say.'

Uncle Alistair munched happily; he did not look at all worried.

'The man at the station,' wondered Maddy, 'what about him?'

'The man on the train,' said Ralph, 'what about him?'

'The man on the train is a mystery,' said Uncle Alistair. 'The man at the station I didn't like the look of at all. It was seeing him that made me decide to keep the case. He didn't look a friendly type to me.'

'And the man on the train jumped when I said "Lower Chernton",' said Maddy. 'I saw him. He said something funny about a girl and a boy being the only way.'

'There you are then,' said Uncle Alistair, as though that settled everything. 'Now, I think you'd both better eat up. I don't want your mothers complaining that I haven't fed you properly.'

When they had finished supper, Uncle Alistair took them for a quick ten-minute saunter by the river. He didn't seem to mind about the washing-up. As they left the house by the side door they could just see the moon fattening in the sky. The river flowed sluggishly past the garden, making a deep, quiet pool. It quickened again as it rushed foamily around the rocks. In the distance they saw a graceful heron stretch his long wings and rise into the star-dusted twilight. It was still warm enough for Maddy and Ralph in their jeans and T-shirts.

'It's so quiet here,' said Ralph, listening.

'That's why I like it,' replied Uncle Alistair. 'There are too many places these days where there's no quiet at all. It's good to come home for a rest.'

He walked to the edge of the river through the long, clinging grass. Tall and lean, he lifted his hands above his head with a loud yawn. Ralph fell to wondering about his uncle again. Where *did* he go? What *did* he do? Uncle Alistair always offered a simple, straightforward explanation, but Ralph had a feeling that the truth was not so simple. It seemed to Ralph now, watching his uncle at the edge of the river, that he almost appeared to grow up from the grass, a part of the countryside. Uncle Alistair was at home with the

21

river, at home with the grass—as though he knew them for what they really were and respected them. That was one of the surprising things about Uncle Alistair. He seemed to know things from the *inside*.

'They may build houses here, you know,' Uncle Alistair said suddenly. He pointed to the empty fields across the river. 'Mr Marlow at the farm may have to sell. He can't make anything pay.'

'That would be a shame,' said Maddy.

'Yes,' said Uncle Alistair thoughtfully, 'it would. They call it progress—but I've never thought progress was piling up more things for people to use.'

'What is it then?' asked Maddy.

Uncle Alistair smiled. 'Progress? Progress is—finding out what's *real*, what's *true* in the world. Then, when you've found out, being changed by it, and living by it! That's something that takes your whole life!'

After a last drink Ralph and Maddy climbed the two flights of stairs to their bedrooms in the attics. Ralph's room was box-like, but not too cramped. Its ceiling slanted in line with the eaves of the house. The small dormer window looked out over the river and the fenced wood. There was an iron bed with a red-striped quilt, a small cupboard painted blue and a wardrobe. A sliver of mirror on one of the wardrobe doors reflected Ralph's image back at himself.

A row of framed pictures leant against the wall. Ralph had to pick his way over cardboard boxes filled with books to get to them. The books were musty and flecked with dust. There were grainy photos in them of past places and past people—Siliguri and Darjeeling, a tea party at Kalimpong. Other, leather-bound books were about Scotland where Granny lived.

At last Ralph curled up in bed and switched off his

bedside light. His back ached a bit. He wanted to sleep, to sleep.

There were sparks in Ralph's dreams that night. Sparks that seemed to fall from the breath of some beast. The autumn smell of burning leaves wafted through the boy's body. And then, in the dark, he felt a pushing, pushing, pushing. Ralph groaned and mumbled to himself. He turned over. Black, oh, how black it was. And the pushing—a thousand hands to push, minds to push, whatever a human being could use to push—whatever the cost, the price, the penalty—those hands were pushing.

Gradually the black began to yield. The black dark threshed in Ralph's dreams and bellowed. Its belly split—painfully—and out of it dropped stars, black stars, that fell screaming into infinite space.

Just as Ralph felt he could bear the terror no longer, he became aware of something that *held*, something strong beneath to catch and keep them safe. Something old, something solid that girdled the earth in its embrace. Something, surely, that would hold?

Ralph wanted to shout a warning. He dived after the stars. When he caught up with them his head hit one and it burst open, spilling a pool of darkness. And in his dream Uncle Alistair was sitting there.

'Uncle Alistair,' said Ralph, 'something terrible's happening. I don't know what it is. It's dark down there and stars are falling and screaming.'

'I've been waiting for you,' was all Uncle Alistair said. He seemed quite calm.

'Really?' said Ralph.

'Oh, for a long time. I want to show you something. Look!'

Uncle Alistair opened the palm of his right hand. There

was a black spot in the middle of it about the size of a penny piece.

'What's that?' asked Ralph.

'It's the darkness,' said Uncle Alistair. 'Don't you recognize it? It's all the darkness you were swimming around in.'

'But it's tiny and it's in your hand,' said Ralph. 'It can't do any harm there.'

'Not *my* hand, Ralph,' said Uncle Alistair, 'you have to understand that.'

And as he said it Ralph trembled. He understood. He knew *whose* hand Uncle Alistair was talking about. The hand that could contain the darkness, that caught the stars, that held the earth. Uncle Alistair was safe in that hand too. He must remember that when the dream—for dream it was—was over.

Ralph groaned—and woke. He opened his eyes to find he had half-crawled from under his quilt.

Ralph had that feeling you have when you know you have dreamed something, but cannot remember what. You try to, you want to—but the more you wake the further away the dream slips, until it's gone. And in a strange bed, in a new place, it took Ralph a few moments to recall where he was.

'I'm at Uncle Alistair's,' he remembered. Then he really woke.

And he heard something outside.

Ralph's reflexes startled his body to wakefulness. He was sure, he was certain, *there was someone in the garden.* He swung his legs out of bed and stumbled in his blue pyjamas to the window. He pinned back the flowery curtain with one hand. The moon had flooded the fields, but the wood remained an impenetrable black. Shapes swirled as Ralph's eyes adjusted to the darkness. He scanned the garden beneath. Nothing. There was nothing. And—no, nothing.

Ralph stayed at the window till his feet grew cold and his arm began to droop. Then there was a scuttle down there, a scrunch of boots and a glint of metal caught by the moon. The figure Ralph briefly saw in the garden was like something out of a picture he had once seen at school. But no, it couldn't be wearing a helmet—surely not! Then it was gone. Chilled now, but still wondering, Ralph took a few strides back to his bed and lay down again to sleep.

'Can I ask you something?' began Maddy. She sat spooning sugar onto her cornflakes. The radio was blaring out news and weather.

'What?'

Uncle Alistair had been up long before Maddy and Ralph came down. He had been sitting in his study poring over his morning mail.

'This house isn't—er—haunted, is it?'

'Certainly not!' Uncle Alistair was offended. 'This is probably the least haunted house in this part of the country.'

'I'm glad to hear it,' mumbled Ralph.

'Ghosts generally don't come near me. They know I don't approve. No one, nothing gets in here.'

'Well, I heard something last night,' said Maddy.

'What was it?'

Uncle Alistair was suddenly interested.

'A kind of knocking. I don't know. It woke me, anyway. It went on for ages.'

'It was probably the pipes. The plumbing in this house is ancient and needs seeing to. One day I'm going to come home and find I've a swimming-pool instead of a kitchen.'

'But I *saw* something!' said Ralph.

'Hmmm?'

Uncle Alistair picked two more slices of brown toast

out of the toaster and put them on the table.

'There was somebody in the garden.'

'Oh, yes?'

Ralph hated not to be listened to, but he hated it much more when he was not believed.

'Perhaps it was a poacher,' Uncle Alistair suggested. 'Men do come to fish the river. I don't mind, though I dare say I should. I know most of them, you see.'

'But . . .' How could Ralph say he thought the man had been wearing a soldier's helmet? 'Oh, forget it.'

'You two have very active imaginations.'

Ralph could have replied—but didn't—that having an uncle like his Uncle Alistair did not help!

'We ought to get out of the house and away from these dark thoughts. It's a lovely day again. Let's take a walk into the village. You two can look around, I have some shopping to do, and then we can have lunch by the river. I have a few things to get on with after that.'

'Great,' said Maddy.

It was hot as they set out. Skylarks sang overhead and the sun fell blindingly on Ralph and Maddy. It seemed much hotter than yesterday. Their shadows were like ink on the road. The trees around them were in the fine, green dress of summer.

'Lovely summer holidays,' said Maddy. 'No school.'

'I never want to go back,' said Ralph.

'One day you won't have to,' said Uncle Alistair, 'then you'll have to go on.' He laughed. 'But don't think it gets any easier.'

At the top end of the village, nearest to Uncle Alistair's, stood the old schoolhouse. A wooden gate opened onto a flagstone path leading up to the front entrance. The schoolhouse had recently been bought by the church for use as a parish hall. Outside a man was hammering up a notice about the summer fête.

'Morning!' greeted Uncle Alistair, not really noticing who it was.

'Mmmm!'

The man mumbled through the nails held between his teeth. He waved his hammer at them.

'Nick Fleming!' said Uncle Alistair. 'What are you doing here? I thought you were in Italy.'

'I'm here for the summer. I'll tell you in a minute. There,' said Nick. He stood back to admire the notice. 'Odd jobs for the vicar. Young Nigel Symmons did that. Talented, don't you think?'

'Without a doubt,' agreed Uncle Alistair.

'Will you be here for the fête this year?'

'Probably ... possibly.'

Ralph caught that tone of voice his mother often used—wanting to appear polite but not wanting to be persuaded to do something.

'I know you're always off somewhere, doing ... something,' said Nick, 'but we need someone— expert—to organize the raffle. Mrs Ward did it last year and I'm not sure her choice of prizes was appreciated by everyone.'

'Oh, I could probably manage that,' said Uncle Alistair.

'Splendid,' Nick beamed.

Nick Fleming had white hair that fell over his forehead. He stooped a little through arthritis. He had retired early, but still worked part-time at the local art college in town. Uncle Alistair lectured there occasionally and the two men had known each other for years.

'That's not really why I stopped you, Alistair,' he went on. 'Something much more exciting—just your sort of thing. We've made a real discovery. That's why I'm here!'

'Really?' Uncle Alistair lifted one eyebrow. 'What is it?'

'It's absolutely marvellous,' Nick enthused, opening the gate. 'You remember Mr Oppenheim?'

'Afraid I don't.'

Nick led them up the path.

'Oh, now I think of it, you wouldn't. He came when you were away in the spring. Mr Oppenheim has become the village benefactor—he's very rich, you see. An American. Well, I don't need to tell you that Lower Chernton, like many other parishes, has been plagued with the costs of restoration and rebuilding. Where is all the money to come from? People are so stretched. And then, where is all the money to go to? You know how the vicar hates pouring money into bricks and mortar when it should be helping people...'

'... so?' said Uncle Alistair, trying to hurry him along.

'Well, that's where Mr Oppenheim comes in. His father made a lot of money selling aeroplanes and his grandmother came from Lower Chernton. So he turns up one day looking for his past, finds the church in need of repair and a hall, and agrees to pay the full cost. What's more, he's stumped up the money to buy the schoolhouse. That keeps it for use by the village instead of being turned into a private house.'

'Well done, Mr Oppenheim!' said Uncle Alistair.

'It was a relief, let me tell you,' said Nick. 'It would have been such a headache raising all the money here. So now the work has started in the church—and here. Just come and see what we've found!'

Uncle Alistair, Maddy and Ralph followed Nick inside. At the entrance was a cloakroom with rows of small pegs for coats. There was a kitchen through a hatch and two airy rooms which had been classrooms. At the far end of the building was the hall. Scaffolding had been erected along one wall. Plastic sheeting was draped over it and brushes stuck out of pots standing at random on the floor.

28

'It's over here,' motioned Nick. 'You see, the school-house was built on the remains of an old priory, and this end of the building is very old. It's a mish-mash of styles, like so many buildings round here, with everything done up and painted over in the nineteenth century.'

Nick pulled aside a white sheet which had been hung up on a string to make a kind of curtain.

'It's rather fascinating, as you'll see.'

Ralph and Maddy crowded closer to see what all the excitement was about. Underneath the plaster, and beginning to show through, were faint colours and patterns—obviously a painting. One end of it had already been uncovered.

'You see?' Nick was jubilant. 'I'm a restorer, after all. This is a find!'

'I do see,' said Uncle Alistair softly. He lifted his hand to brush the painting. Ragged bits of plaster still stuck to it and the whole was coated with a thick, floury dust.

'I'm in charge of this,' said Nick, 'so I've moved into my cottage for the duration. It means I'll be here all the time instead of just at weekends. It shouldn't take long to uncover the rest of it.'

'I hope not. You're right, it is most interesting.'

The painting revealed so far showed two knights on horseback. One rode a black horse, and one a white. The knight on the white horse held his lance raised and was dressed in full armour. The ground beneath the horses' hooves was curled into a pattern of gold which flowed mysteriously into the remaining plaster on the wall.

'Medieval?' enquired Uncle Alistair.

'We think so,' Nick said.

'And local?'

'It's possible,' replied Nick.

'It has to be, surely?' said Uncle Alistair. 'Where's your local history, Nick? Aren't there four horsemen who appear around these parts whenever there's trouble? You've found only two as yet, but there's more of the picture to come.'

'Of course! I just hadn't thought. I've been more concerned about uncovering the painting without damaging it.'

'Who are they?' asked Maddy. 'What horsemen?'

'A local story,' said Nick. 'Nothing famous. A troupe of knights from hereabouts went off to fight in the Crusades. That was in the thirteenth century. Years later, four of them came back—the rest had been slaughtered. When the knights came home the castle was in ruins and there was nothing left for them here. As the only survivors they pledged to do good and fight evil wherever they could find it.'

'And they did,' interrupted Uncle Alistair. 'They became quite well-known—a bit like Robin Hood—only they defended people, they didn't rob the rich to give to the poor. The story was written down in an old chronicle. After a few years of this, one of them had a dream or a kind of vision. In it he was told that the four knights had been charged to guard something of great value for which they would need all their strength and skill. None of the knights understood the dream, but they all wondered what they had been chosen to do.

'One afternoon, out hunting, they chased a white hind which led them over the countryside. The hind ran into the hollow of a hill near here and the four knights followed. With that they vanished and were never heard of again. Only, the story is that they did not die. Instead, they lie sleeping. Now and then, in time of great peril, they wake up and ride forth once more to do good.'

'Has anyone ever seen them?' Ralph was serious.

Nick laughed. 'Some people say so, but the knights haven't appeared for a long time now.'

'The last sighting was reported by Millie Rawlings in 1873,' said Uncle Alistair.

'Really? How did you dig that out?' Nick Fleming looked amazed.

'I like local history.' Uncle Alistair's face cracked into a grin. 'I like finding out the things no one else can be bothered with. You ought to know that by now! Millie Rawlings was a parlourmaid at the Grange. Don't you know the story, Nick? Her mother was ill and she had been allowed to go and visit her. As she was walking back that night two men tried to attack her—near that mound by Marlow's farm. Naturally, she screamed for help. Suddenly, a man on horseback appeared out of the wood and brandished a sword. He rode straight at the two men, who ran off. So Millie was safe. The villagers were convinced that one of the four sleeping horsemen had woken and come to her rescue.'

'Well, it's a good story, anyway.' Nick chuckled approvingly. 'But I must get back to work. About the Grange, though...' his forehead creased with a frown. 'You know Sir James died last month? He was an old widower, childless, popular with everyone. The brownies and cubs were always round there, running all over the place. He did a lot of money-raising, sat on most of the local committees, always opened the fête...'

'Yes, I often used to visit him—before he was too ill.'

'Well, the Grange has passed to Sir James' nephew now—Sir George. And he's quite another cup of tea. He won't have anything to do with the village. He's more or less locked himself up at the Grange. I bumped into him for the first time the other day and—it's odd, but—I found him rather frightening.'

'Frightening?'

'There's just something about him, driving around in that black car of his. And he has the strangest visitors.

They come and go and we don't see them much in the village. They give me the shivers. People are beginning to ask what's going on at the Grange. But I must get back to work...'

'I didn't realize Sir George had moved in already,' said Uncle Alistair. They were out of the schoolhouse gate now, and walking into the village.

'He doesn't sound very nice,' said Maddy.

'Where's the Grange?' asked Ralph.

'Over there.' Uncle Alistair indicated a high wall smothered in a tumble of ivy. The top half of the house was just visible, through a line of beech trees inside the wall.

The Grange was not huge, but it had extensive grounds. The sun glinted on its many windows. It was quite separate from the other houses in the village—and closest to the schoolhouse.

Uncle Alistair, Ralph and Maddy walked on down the High Street. Cars were parked along the kerb and morning shoppers were out.

'You won't want to shop,' Uncle Alistair said. 'I'll meet you here in fifteen minutes.' He strode off down the street towards the small supermarket.

'Well,' said Maddy, 'what do you think?'

But before Ralph could give a proper answer, he pointed: 'Look!' Gliding down the High Street came a large black limousine with darkened glass windows. 'That must be Sir George's car. It fits Nick's description. It couldn't be anyone else's.'

The car halted, with its engine still purring, quite close to them. The man who climbed out seemed vaguely familiar. He was wearing a black jacket and dark sunglasses. As he waited for the car to drive away, his penetrating gaze took in the length of the street. His presence among the shoppers on the pavement seemed to spread some kind of chill. People instinctively moved to one side to let him through.

'Do you reckon that's the man from the railway station?' asked Maddy.

'I think so. Come on, let's have a closer look.'

'I don't know that I want to.'

The man halted in front of the butcher's. Liver and kidney and sausages lay in white trays in the window. Prices were daubed in paint on the glass below the pulled-up venetian blinds.

'I'm sure he's looking at us.' Maddy tugged Ralph's arm.

'Don't be silly! He doesn't know who we are.'

'How do we know *what* he knows? He could know anything. Oh!'

Maddy did not need to point. Coming out of the post office on the other side of the road was a woman. She was wearing a long red-and-gold skirt and black sandals. Her hair was tied back in a pony tail so long that it flicked at her waist. She was heavily made up, with thick green eyeshadow. She waited a moment for the traffic to pass and began to cross the street.

'I bet I know who she's going to talk to,' said Ralph.

They watched, mesmerized, as she approached the man in the black jacket and placed one hand on his shoulder. The two began to talk, heads together, but glancing up each time someone passed.

Ralph let out a long whistle.

'So they're Sir George's friends! No wonder they gave Nick the shivers! What a pair!'

'Let's find Uncle Alistair,' said Maddy. 'I don't want to wait here.'

'OK.'

They edged up the pavement to pass the strange couple. The woman's face was pale and her eyes were heavy. As they passed, Maddy caught a whiff of the woman's perfume. It was very unusual. It was . . . Maddy remembered now —she was good at remembering smells. It was what the man on the train's tobacco smell had been mixed up with! The man with the suitcase!

'Are they following us?' asked Maddy in a whisper.

'I don't think so,' said Ralph, 'but they *are* coming this way.'

'What if he recognizes us from the station? What if he thinks we have the suitcase?'

'Why should he know anything about the suitcase?'

Maddy halted. She was confused. Somehow it had seemed an obvious connection to make.

'Here!'

Ralph swung open a shop door just as Uncle Alistair emerged with a plastic carrier bag full of lunch.

'What's all this?' he asked, seeing the alarm on their faces.

'Them!' exclaimed Maddy, pointing.

Uncle Alistair stared down the street. The man and the woman had stopped again. They were huddled over the cashpoint outside the bank.

'So you've found company,' he said thoughtfully.

'They're company I'd like to lose,' said Maddy firmly.

'Maybe so,' said Uncle Alistair, 'but what if they're company that's found you?'

With that he turned, swinging the plastic bag, and set off back up the High Street.

3

Uncle Alistair sprawled on the picnic rug, absorbed in peeling an orange. Ralph sat throwing stones into the river. They fell with a hollow plop into the pool. Maddy gazed up at the sky and the few blobs of cloud passing overhead.

'I'm worried about Sir George's friends,' Uncle Alistair said.

'Oh, why?' Ralph continued throwing stones. He tried to skim a flat one across the pool.

'Why do you think?'

Maddy sat up and reached for a chocolate biscuit. 'I can see why your friend Nick doesn't like them,' she said.

'Why do you think they all turn up at the Grange?' asked Ralph.

'I suppose that's for us to find out,' replied Uncle Alistair. He sighed and began dissecting his orange into segments. He gazed across the water. The air was full of the sounds of the countryside.

Ralph was suddenly aware that his clothes smelled of juicy grass. He looked over the river towards the sweep of the wood on the other side. The trees loomed together so that only a dappled, undersea glimmer of light showed through the leaves. Where the wood ended, fields began. He could see Mr Marlow's farmhouse and, in the distance, an unploughed mound planted with a ring of trees.

As Ralph watched he had a strange sensation. Just a faint tingling at first. He rubbed his left arm and pulled it in to his side. But instead of going away, the tingling grew, stronger, faster. Ralph blinked hard. The trees, the hills tipping up to the sky, the sloping fields, everything around him, seemed to be pressed together. They were all being pressed as if by the squeezing palm of some giant. He blinked nervously. He saw, or thought he saw, the trees leaning over. They were like glass, their leaves almost transparent. Behind, beyond, lay the hint of something else, something infinite. This something was drawing closer. It was like the pushing in Ralph's dream. Something was happening. Behind the afternoon, there rose something ... endless ...

Ralph shook himself. A cloud rolled its heavy shadow over the riverbank. Uncle Alistair quickly looked up at Ralph.

'I think we should go in now,' he said.

Back home, Uncle Alistair put the cups and plates into the sink and turned the tap on. Suddenly, the phone rang.

'See who that is, will you, Maddy?' he asked.

Maddy went out into the hall and picked up the receiver. 'Hello?' she said.

There was a click and then she heard the dialling tone. 'Funny,' she murmured.

'Who was it?' called Uncle Alistair from the kitchen.

Before Maddy could answer, the phone gave another ring. Maddy picked it up, but the same thing happened.

'No one,' she said, puzzled.

'No one! Nothing! This will drive us mad!' Uncle Alistair said from the kitchen. 'Somebody and something would make a welcome change!'

No one. Nothing. Suddenly Maddy realized that the suitcase had been on her mind all afternoon. She walked into the front room to have a look at it again. It was still by the fireplace. The twin snakes, gold and intriguing, circled endlessly on the lid. Maddy picked it up and sat with it resting on her knees. The snakes—Maddy had not noticed it before but the snakes with their tails tucked into their mouths looked as though they were—in a way—giving birth to themselves. Maddy traced them with her finger. On and on, in an endless round they circled, endlessly giving birth and endlessly swallowing themselves. It didn't make sense: the snakes seemed to be creating and destroying themselves at the same time.

Maddy stroked the case thoughtfully. She clicked open the locks. Her blood beat at the sharp sound. She lifted the lid of the case.

Inside, it was the same as before. A deep, wide darkness lay at the bottom of the case. There was nothing, just Nothing. As she had seen Ralph do, she reached inside with her arm. There was no hot, no cold, no sensation at all—just . . . Nothing. Maddy drew back her arm and gazed into the formless depths of the case. As she stared, a strange feeling washed over her—the feeling you have when you are standing high up, on top of a castle or a tower. You look down—and you want to jump off. That was exactly how Maddy felt now. The case seemed to call her, invite her, will her to throw herself in. The blackness opened like a warm mouth. 'Come!' it said. She shivered. 'Come!' it repeated.

Maddy moved closer and felt the darkness surge through her. She leant forward—and swam into Nothing.

'Maddy! Maddy!' A faraway voice echoed through her head.

'What?' she replied.

The voice had no body. It came from far away, distant, as if through sheets of ice which had taken centuries to freeze.

'Maddy! No!' the voice shouted.

In the darkness a pinpoint of light seemed to be coming towards her. She tried to focus her eyes. Then she saw that the light had human form. It was Uncle Alistair. He was calm, controlling his urgency.

'This way, Maddy,' said the voice, so firm and gentle that it made you want to obey it.

Uncle Alistair raised his hand. With one hacking motion he seemed to shear the darkness into shreds that fell before him.

'Don't be afraid! Follow the light, Maddy,' he said. 'Don't take your eyes off the light!'

Maddy obeyed. She didn't want to get lost. There was darkness all around her.

At first Maddy thought the light was coming from Uncle Alistair. But then she realized it wasn't. The light was coming *through* him from somewhere else. This Somewhere Else made Maddy gasp even to think about it. For the light was like beautiful music. It played in her head. And the notes formed a ladder to help her feet. The light was like spring, giving new life—life so strong, so deep it could run right through the world if only the world would let it—a life which would never end.

'This way,' said Uncle Alistair. Her hand was in his strong grasp now. 'This is the way. Follow the light!' And the darkness ebbed away, defeated.

Uncle Alistair shut the lid of the case with a snap.

'Maddy! Maddy!' he said.

Maddy heard a loud singing in her ears. She felt chilled by the darkness and drawn to the light. She was still hovering far away, as if someone had come and pulled her out of her body.

'Oh!' she heard herself saying. There was a rush of blood to her cheeks. 'What happened? What happened?'

'I think we should keep this thing shut from now on.'

Uncle Alistair said firmly. 'Do not open it again *under any circumstances*, do you hear?'

Ralph appeared timidly at the door.

'And that goes for you, too!' he added.

Maddy nodded. She was still not wholly sure where she was or *what* had actually happened.

Uncle Alistair sat on the sofa beside her. Slowly she came back to herself. 'That was quite dangerous, you know,' he said, and then, in a much gentler voice, 'You must be careful.' Even when he was gentle there was something unshakeable about Uncle Alistair. As if his feet were set on rock.

'I—I think I'm better now.' Maddy stammered. 'What happened?'

'You almost fell into Nothing and I had to come after you. Sit still and wait till you feel better. Ralph, I think you'd better leave Maddy on her own for a while. Why don't you go for a walk by the river?'

At bedtime Maddy stood brushing her teeth in her bedroom. She shivered to think about what had happened. She turned on the basin tap and the flow of water set the pipes in the wall knocking. Maddy looked at herself in the mirror above the basin. She was pale and tired. She heard a creak outside on the landing. It must be Ralph. Maddy opened the door to say goodnight. But it was not Ralph. There was no one there. The landing light was off.

From her bedroom door Maddy could see Ralph's door. It was closed. The light from her room spilled out onto the landing, and onto the stairwell which led down to the middle floor. Glancing out, Maddy saw a large, balloon-like shadow on the stairwell opposite. She slipped out, barefoot, to see who it was. What she caught was a flash, just a flash, of someone—a figure in black in a maid's starched apron and cap carrying a silver tray. Maddy backed into her room and sat down on the edge of her bed. She clasped her hands. Was she starting to imagine things?

Ralph woke. Maddy woke. It was after three. Neither knew anything about the other. Maddy lay in bed. She heard a colossal crack of thunder and the hiss and spit and drum of heavy rain on the roof. The earth seemed to sigh. It needed rain, this dry summer. The farmers had started complaining. Too much heat. But farmers always grumbled, Uncle Alistair said. They always wanted rain or sun to order. Crack, a flash of light—and the sound of heavy rain. But as Maddy looked towards the window she saw no rain on the glass. No drips from the gutter outside.

Ralph was standing at his window. He could see no rain, he just heard the heavy constant hiss of it. The ground in Uncle Alistair's garden was dry. The trees in the wood were barely moving. There was a flash again and the drumming rain-drops on the roof grew even louder.

Maddy saw it happen. She too was standing by the window. A flash and a flame. She pulled back the curtains. A tree at the edge of the lawn had been struck by lightning. As she watched, it fell like a slain giant. Its branches crackled in painful dissolving flame. The trunk slumped across the fence like a wounded body. The thunder was like gunshot in the air. It shook the unseen sky. But no rain fell and the night was still. The window-panes remained dry. Outside, there was—after all—only a warm, peaceful summer's night.

'It was an interesting night,' remarked Uncle Alistair the following morning. He was sitting on the sofa in the living-room, reading a newspaper.

Both Maddy and Ralph shot him an irritated look. 'Interesting' was not how either of them would have described it.

Uncle Alistair folded his paper. 'Did you sleep well?' he asked, with a lift of his eyebrows.

'No,' said Ralph.

'No,' said Maddy. She yawned as though to prove the point.

'Neither did I . . . much.'

'There was a thunderstorm,' began Maddy.

'Oh, you heard that, did you?'

Ralph nodded in silent agreement.

'And a maid on the stairs,' said Maddy. 'At least, I think she was a maid.' She stood behind the sofa with her arms folded.

Uncle Alistair turned to look at Maddy. 'Yes, I heard someone prowling around and had to come down,' he said. 'I think I saw a black collie dog in the kitchen. But I couldn't be sure. You can never be sure of these things.'

'And a tree fell,' continued Maddy. 'In the garden. It was struck by lightning.'

'Ah, now, *that's* interesting,' said Uncle Alistair.

'Why?'

'Go and have a look.'

Maddy walked over to the bay window and stared out. There was no tree at the edge of the lawn. Beside the fence there was just grass—as if there had never been a tree there.

'I bought this house from Colonel Stanley,' Uncle Alistair explained. 'That was about fifteen years ago. He told me about a thunderstorm in the fifties when a tree came down in the garden. It sounded as though that was quite a night!'

'What are you saying?' Ralph butted in. 'Are you saying that was the *same* thunderstorm last night—that it had happened before?'

'Well, what did you see, Maddy?'

'I saw the tree falling. It was on fire. It fell across the fence.'

'There you go!' Uncle Alistair sat back.

But Ralph wasn't satisfied. 'A thunderstorm without rain?' he demanded. 'What's going on?'

Uncle Alistair put his newspaper down and crossed his legs. He took a deep breath. 'In my opinion,' he said very seriously, 'somebody is playing with time.'

'Time?' echoed Maddy.

'That's what I said. Time is important stuff, you know. If we didn't have time to do things in, nothing would exist at all.'

'But how can you play with time?' asked Maddy. 'I thought time just ... happened ...'

'So it does, for the most part.'

Uncle Alistair laced his slim fingers in front of him and stared down at them.

'As far as we are concerned, time is fixed,' he said. 'There are rules and laws governing time just as there are rules and laws for everything else. But Einstein ... you've heard of him? Well, Einstein showed that time could move faster or slower depending on how fast or how slowly you were moving yourself. After that, scientists had to change the way they thought about time. In fact, they had to change their whole way of thinking about how the universe works.

'But time isn't only scientific, you see—it also has to do with *experience*. What happens to us today and what happened yesterday all happens in time. Sometimes time seems to drag, other times it flies by. The clock continues to tick at the same rate, but we seem to be living at different speeds, as though we were carried by the eddies and currents of a river. Time is a complicated affair!'

'So?' asked Ralph. 'What's that got to do with last night?'

'Well, it's possible that the thunderstorm was an echo of something that happened here long ago,' continued

Uncle Alistair. 'I don't believe for a moment that we travelled back in time. What we had was a glimpse of the past in the present.' Uncle Alistair leaned forward excitedly. 'Now, if bits of the past are suddenly popping up in the present and we are seeing them and hearing them—some kind of disturbance of time must be going on. That's not *natural*—far from it—and there may be a dark purpose behind it. I think someone is tampering with the fabric of time.'

'Who?' asked Ralph blankly. 'And how, and why?'

Before Uncle Alistair could answer, the phone in the hall began ringing. 'Oh, that phone!' Uncle Alistair tutted. 'It'll probably be Gail saying that she can't come on Thursday. She and her family are off to Spain at the weekend.'

Uncle Alistair went out to the hall but was back almost immediately.

'Nobody,' he said. 'Isn't that interesting!'

'I'm worried,' said Maddy. 'I don't think it's interesting at all.'

'I didn't say I wasn't worried, but it *is* interesting. Why should someone keep ringing us and then put down the phone the moment we answer?'

'Maybe they're just checking we're here?' Ralph snorted. He was hungry. He wanted his breakfast.

'You're right, Ralph. Or maybe they want to find out when we're *not* here.'

Maddy looked alarmed. 'The suitcase!' she exclaimed.

'Possibly . . .' Uncle Alistair was thoughtful. 'I need to go to the bank this morning and I would rather you two came with me. Before we go out I think we should make sure that wretched suitcase is well and truly hidden. But first—breakfast!'

'This is a secret!' They were in Uncle Alistair's bedroom. He opened the wardrobe door and removed some boards from the back. Hidden behind his wardrobe was a large metal safe with a combination lock. With careful, precise movements Uncle Alistair turned the dial. Inside the safe were a number of bundles tied up with cloth and some very old books. There was plenty of room for the case.

'It should be safe enough here,' said Uncle Alistair. He closed the heavy door, turned the combination knob, put the boards back in place and shut the wardrobe.

'There!' He wiped the dust off his hands. 'Now,' he smiled, 'are you ready to go?'

It was even hotter than yesterday. They walked slowly in the stifling heat towards the village.

'The temperature just seems to go up and up!' said Uncle Alistair.

As they turned the corner into the High Street by the schoolhouse, they heard a voice shouting, 'Hey!' It was Nick Fleming, waving wildly as he ran from the schoolhouse towards them. 'I'm glad I caught you!' he said breathlessly. He looked anxious.

'What is it?' asked Uncle Alistair.

'I wish I knew,' he replied. 'It may be more your kind of thing. Come and see!'

Ralph, Maddy and Uncle Alistair followed Nick into the schoolhouse. Inside, beams of sunlight spread across the dark wood of the floorboards from the high, pointed windows. The thick stone walls made it quiet and cool.

'What do you make of this?' said Nick. 'It's extraordinary!'

He pulled back the white sheet from the medieval wall painting. A third horseman was now beginning to show through the peeling plaster. Nick had been hard at work. But Ralph and Maddy understood at once why he was so concerned.

'It's moved!' Maddy gaped at the painting.

'Indeed it has,' said Uncle Alistair softly.

Ralph sniffed. A smell of damp like decomposing leaves hung in the air. It almost seemed to be oozing through the wall. The knight riding the white horse had moved. His lance was now thrust in front of him. The horse he rode was beginning to rear as though he were about to gallop into an attack.

'Astonishing!' exclaimed Uncle Alistair.

'Isn't it?' said Nick, his voice trembling. 'I don't know how I'm going to explain it.'

'Well,' said Uncle Alistair, stroking his chin, 'I would wait . . . after all, the painting isn't fully uncovered yet. Wait until you get the complete picture . . .'

Nick looked relieved. 'I'm glad you're around, Alistair. You don't go off the deep end the minute something unusual happens. And there are some strange things happening at the moment.'

'Oh?' asked Uncle Alistair casually.

Nick spoke in a low voice in the way grown-ups do when they think children can't hear. Ralph and Maddy tried to look very hard at the painting, all the time listening to what was being said.

'People in the village have been seeing and hearing things,' said Nick. 'One woman claims she saw a soldier standing in her kitchen. Another says she heard a thunderstorm last night, but there wasn't any rain. What do you make of it?'

'I've no idea,' replied Uncle Alistair lightly. Ralph and Maddy continued to stare up at the painting, their ears burning.

'Well,' Nick chuckled, 'it'd do some of them good to be shaken up a bit.' Then he was serious again. 'But I don't like it. Nobody does. Not at all . . . and this . . .' he gestured towards the painting, 'and the heat. What do you think I should do?'

'I'd say keep quiet,' replied Uncle Alistair. 'Carry on with the restoration and report any developments. Tell everyone that your work is at a delicate stage and keep it covered. Say that the painting shouldn't be exposed to light on any account, otherwise it might be damaged. Who knows, that might be true.'

'I'll do that,' said Nick. 'No need to get everyone upset. And I'll keep you informed.'

Uncle Alistair strode down the High Street, deep in thought. Maddy and Ralph followed him, longing to talk about the painting. After Uncle Alistair came out of the bank, he said, 'I have to go to the post office and send this to Tsering in India. Won't be a minute.'

Mrs Symmons, who worked behind the counter, was the mother of young Nigel who had designed the poster for the fête. Uncle Alistair greeted her warmly.

'Funny business going on,' she said, 'and the heat doesn't help.' And she started to tell Uncle Alistair something in a whisper.

Ralph and Maddy lingered near the door beside the shelves of magazines and newspapers.

' . . . then . . .' said a woman who was at the shop end of the post office, 'I didn't know what to think!'

'No,' the shopkeeper agreed absent-mindedly. He was obviously used to the endless chatter of this particular customer.

'I told Geoff, but he thought I was seeing things. Said it was too much television! As though I have time to watch television! But I'll swear blind—I got home and there were three children running round the kitchen table! No shoes or anything, and so dirty. I thought they were something out of a film at first, or playing tricks. "What are you doing here?" I asked. And then, you won't believe it, but they *weren't* there, they just *weren't* there. I was flummoxed, I can tell you! It gave me quite a turn! I had to sit down and have a cup of tea. But how do you get anybody to believe you? I've heard of things like that happening—but to other people. I never thought that anything like that would happen to me!'

'No . . .' said the shopkeeper wearily, taking her money and giving her the change.

'I mean to say,' the woman went on, 'if it's happened once, what will happen next? Who knows *what* the house will be full of when I get home?'

'Oh, I agree.' The shopkeeper made sympathetic noises as the woman put her shopping into her bag and walked out.

Ralph and Maddy followed her to the heat of the pavement outside.

'Did you hear all that?' Ralph asked.

'Of course I did,' said Maddy. 'I don't know whether to be glad it's not only us, or to be more frightened.'

They both sat down on the step, looking at the ground. A blue and white striped awning took the glare of the sun off the shop windows. A dog snuffled around a waste bin by the kerb. Then a pair of black shoes stepped by the bin. They heard the sound of a match being struck as a cigarette was lit. The dog yelped and darted round the bin, scampering away.

Maddy and Ralph looked up. The man with the cigarette was fair and thin. From where they sat he appeared young. But on closer inspection his face was lined and hollowed as though something had been sucked out of it. There was something . . . absent . . . missing . . . about him. The man's hair hung limp: it was receding from his forehead. His shoulders were hunched.

The man dropped a few papers from his trouser pocket into the bin and moved on up the High Street, going into the bank.

'What do you bet that's Sir George?' asked Ralph.

'Ugh!' said Maddy. 'If that was him, I didn't like the look of him at all!'

'Now, you two!' Uncle Alistair appeared behind them. 'It's time we were getting back! I've got some stuff for lunch. We can have it outside.' He swung a bulging carrier bag. 'Come on,' he said. 'While we still have time.'

When they reached the house, the gate to the drive was unfastened. It had swung away from the post just a little, but that was enough. Uncle Alistair gripped the top bar.

'Somebody's been here!'

'Maybe you left it open yourself?' said Maddy.

'No, it's not that. Somebody's been here. I can sort of ... feel it! Hold on!'

Uncle Alistair hurried up the drive. For all Ralph and Maddy could tell, the house appeared untouched.

'Come on!' urged Ralph. He and Maddy ran after Uncle Alistair, as he opened the front door and disappeared inside.

'Oh, no!' Uncle Alistair groaned. 'Don't look—no— come and look! You'll have to, anyway!'

Maddy and Ralph followed him into the hall. Confusion greeted them. The phone was dangling helplessly and the books had been emptied from the shelves. Papers lay scattered over the front room. Drawers had been pulled out and overturned. Water from the flower vases was dripping onto the floor.

'How on earth did they have the time?' muttered Uncle Alistair.

There was that word again. Time. It bored its way into Ralph's mind. Time. How could people find time and lose time? What did it mean to 'have time', Ralph wondered? You couldn't own time, not like a possession, not like a car or a watch. He had never really thought about time before.

Why was it so bad to play around with time? Why were people seeing things?

'Don't touch anything!' ordered Uncle Alistair. He picked up the phone and began to dial. 'I'd better call the police.' Uncle Alistair was dismal and resigned. 'As you can see, we've been well and truly burgled.'

Distracted by the mess downstairs, they completely forgot the suitcase.

4

Ralph, Maddy and Uncle Alistair went to sit on the lawn overlooking the river. They had been asked to touch nothing until the police arrived.

'Who could have broken in?' asked Ralph, as they began to eat.

'Almost anybody,' sighed Uncle Alistair. He lay resting on his elbows, munching a cheese roll.

'*Almost* anybody?'

Uncle Alistair didn't answer. 'Once the police have been we can tidy up and see if the burglars have taken anything,' he said.

'Don't you have an alarm?' asked Ralph. 'Lots of people do.'

Uncle Alistair laughed softly. 'I don't usually need an alarm. It's a mistake to think that anybody can go anywhere, you know. Some places are protected. No ordinary burglar would have been able to come into this house.'

'But who could have done it?' Ralph frowned.

'Sir George?' Maddy uttered the name in both their minds.

Uncle Alistair shook his head. 'Why would Sir George break into my house?'

'We saw him in the village!' Ralph sat up, excited.

'Sir George? But you don't even know what he looks like!'

'Well . . .' Maddy began carefully, finishing a chocolate

biscuit. 'We saw somebody who didn't look like anybody else in the village. Somehow he looked like that man and woman we saw in the High Street yesterday. So we thought he must be Sir George.'

Uncle Alistair laughed. 'I see! A fine pair of detectives you would make! You have to have hard evidence before you go round saying that people are who you think they are. That man might have been somebody completely different!'

'Are feelings evidence?' asked Ralph. 'Because my feelings say we saw Sir George.'

'Not in a court of law ... But maybe you are right. Maybe you did see Sir George. I wonder.'

'What are you thinking?'

Uncle Alistair plucked a daisy. He held its brilliant petals a few inches from his face, studying it intensely.

'It seems a strange coincidence to me ... that you two should stumble across Sir George the very moment the house is being burgled. If the man in the village *was* Sir George. Of course, on the face of it, you could easily have bumped into Sir George at any time. But it's not on the face of it that we need to look. We need to find out what's really going on. And I'm worried there's a lot going on.'

'But then,' said Ralph, 'he has an alibi! If we saw him in the village, he couldn't have been here, could he?'

'Morning!' A loud voice called from the drive. They heard a bicycle being parked against the wall.

'That'll be PC Cook,' said Uncle Alistair. 'He doesn't have very many burglaries to deal with.'

PC Cook had brought a notebook, but he asked only a few questions. 'I'll have to ring into town,' he decided almost at once. 'We don't get much of this sort of thing round here, you know.'

Uncle Alistair was irritated all of a sudden. 'That's why I

moved into the village. I thought I could get away from . . .
things . . .'

'Do you mind if I use the phone?'

About an hour later a detective drove in from town
with another policeman. He and Uncle Alistair went into
the house. Maddy and Ralph followed. The detective took
off his tweed jacket and rolled up his shirt sleeves. He was
quite young and had a beard.

After taking down a lot of details he asked, 'What's
been taken?'

'I don't know. I doubt if anything's been taken.'

'Why? Haven't you . . .?'

'No, I haven't cleared up, as you can see. I was asked not
to till you came,' said Uncle Alistair shortly.

'Yes, that was the right thing to do. Why do you think
nothing's been taken?'

'Because I don't own anything valuable—not in that
sense, anyway. Besides, all the obvious things which
could have been stolen are still in place.'

Uncle Alistair waved his hand round the disordered
room. He was right. Everything that by rights should
have been stolen was still there—the paintings on the
wall, the ornaments and the old TV had not been touched.

'Funny business.' The detective made a few notes on his
pad, then rose to leave. 'Let us know if you turn up any
clues . . .' He shook Uncle Alistair's hand.

The two officers got into their car and bumped down
the drive.

'That's that, then!' Uncle Alistair turned towards
Maddy and Ralph. 'It doesn't sound very hopeful. But
at least we can tidy up. I'll ring Gail and see if she can come
and help. Then we'll have a conference.'

Gail smiled warmly as she was introduced to Maddy

and Ralph. But her smile soon faded when she saw the living-room.

'I never expected anything like this to happen here.' She was evidently shaken. 'Never. It's always felt so safe.'

Gail cleaned up in the hall. She washed the floor and hung a couple of rugs out to dry. She picked up the scattered flowers and rearranged them. And gradually they moved from room to room, tidying up. The bedrooms upstairs had all been entered (all the doors were wide open), but left untouched. Whatever the burglars had been after, they clearly did not think they would find it up there.

Down in the living-room Uncle Alistair sorted piles of papers, then went into his study to deal with the files and drawers. Maddy and Ralph arranged the books, but Uncle Alistair insisted on looking at each one before it went back to its proper home on the shelves.

'You never know,' he explained, 'one thing could have been taken, only one thing you would never notice, and it might be the most vital, the most important thing of all.'

'I think,' announced Gail, popping her head round the door at last, 'I've finished now.' The afternoon had more or less gone. 'I'm glad they didn't touch the kitchen or I'd have been all night!' she added.

'Thank you for coming, Gail.'

'No problem—I don't think I can manage Thursday, though.'

'I didn't expect you to. Have a good holiday!'

'Thanks, and keep away from burglars!'

'We'll do our best!'

Ralph, however, did not quite believe his uncle. He knew that Uncle Alistair was determined to get to the bottom of what had happened and find out who had entered the house.

Uncle Alistair prowled round the front room checking

everything. The problem is, once you have been burgled, even if nothing has been taken and everything is back exactly in the same place, you *know* somebody has been there, and you *know* whoever it was can come again.

'I need to take measures,' muttered Uncle Alistair. 'This mustn't happen again. Ralph, there's a red box in the cupboard under the stairs. Could you go and get it?'

Ralph found the box on a shelf.

'What's in it?'

'Open it and see.'

The wooden box was packed with white candles.

'Candles?' Ralph pulled a face. .

'That's right.' Uncle Alistair went to a drawer and took out some candleholders. He laid them on the table.

'What on earth are you doing?' asked Ralph.

' "We", Ralph, "we". We're in this together. We're going to put candles round the rooms.'

'Is this a "measure"?' asked Ralph. 'How will candles stop anything?'

'Hush! Don't let your mind run on so quickly.' Uncle Alistair started to put the candles into the candleholders and gestured to Maddy to help him. He set them in place around the room, and then told Ralph and Maddy to put two candles in every room of the house.

'What's the point of all this?' asked Maddy, returning to the living-room.

'Think,' said Uncle Alistair. 'What do candles do?'

'They burn,' said Ralph.

'And . . .'

Maddy shrugged. 'They give off light.'

'Exactly! They give off light. We could do with some light just now. I'd like some light on this burglary, for a start.'

'But how will candles help?'

'If I light a candle in a dark room, what happens?' asked Uncle Alistair.

'You can see,' said Ralph.

'And what happens to the darkness?'

'It vanishes.'

Uncle Alistair looked thoughtful. 'We are in the midst of some great darkness right now, Ralph. I don't know what it is, but I do know it's there and that it's growing stronger. What we need is light to beat back that darkness. No, more than that! The darkness must disappear, or who knows what the consequences will be! No ordinary burglar came into this house today...'

'... but *candles*?' said Maddy.

'Think of them as a picture,' Uncle Alistair said. 'People talk a lot about light—the light of goodness and truth which is there for everyone. But that is no more than a faint glimmer of the real Light—the Light that calls each one of us to follow absolutely—though only a few ever recognize it.

'That Light can defeat any darkness, however great. It *has* defeated Darkness already, though there are still those who prowl around, eaten up by their own darkness and ready to destroy what they can to gain what they want. They are blind to the Light and do not understand it. They hate it. They wish they could put it out, but they can't—so they try to put it out in the people who do have it.

'There was a time when it looked as though the Light *had* been put out, but it returned to burn all the more strongly. The world has never been the same since, nor can it be—for the Light is in the world, calling everyone home to itself.'

It came to Ralph that his uncle was talking in a kind of code, to help them understand. The real words would have been too much for them. Uncle Alistair was like that. He gave you only what you could take—a little at a time.

And the candles. Ralph looked at them arranged round the room, and now he saw them with new eyes. He imagined them burning against the dark windows, their flames combined into one flame, into one Light against which the darkness could not prevail.

Abruptly, Ralph's thoughts returned to the burglar. 'Is anything missing?' he asked.

'Yes, I'm afraid so.'

'What is it?' Maddy had not noticed anything. Nothing *obvious* had gone.

'A book.'

'The burglars made all that mess for just one book?'

'Not just a book, Ralph. No book is *just* a book. Besides, this was a special book.'

'What kind of book was it?'

Uncle Alistair hesitated. 'A book of local history.'

'Why would anyone take a book like that?'

'Last century there was a man in the village called Sir William Fenton, the great-great-grandfather of our Sir George. He spent many years of his life researching and digging things up. He interviewed old people round here to collect their stories. He eventually wrote a book called *The Chernton Chronicle* which was privately published in 1894. Only fifty copies were ever printed. I have one and the town library has one, but nobody else around here does. Ihe funny thing is, the book was given me as a special present many years ago.'

'Who gave it to you?'

'Sir James at the Grange—the old man who died recently. The man Nick Fleming was talking about.'

'Sir George's uncle!'

'That's right, Maddy—Sir George's uncle.'

'But why would anyone take a book like that?'

'I don't know, but Sir William Fenton's book has one special feature that makes it rather unusual. It's a particular local legend. Not the horsemen, another one.'

'What's it about?'

'It's the legend of Aelfric.'

'Aelfric? Who was Aelfric?' The name meant nothing to Ralph.

'He lived long ago in what we now call the Dark Ages: after the Romans left—before Britain became a single country. In those days the land was divided into small tribes and kingdoms. Aelfric was known as the Black Warrior because he was always dressed in black. He ruled in these parts and the local people feared him. He did terrible things and was without mercy.

'One day, a wandering saint called Benedictus arrived from across the sea. Aelfric had heard he could cure people and thought he was a wizard—though he wasn't, of course. Aelfric saw this powerful saint as a rival and challenged him to a duel.

'Benedictus refused to fight. Aelfric grew angry and tried to strike him with his sword—but the saint only laughed and told Aelfric he would give him a chance to mend his ways. Then he struck the side of the hill they were standing on with his staff. After three knocks a door opened in the hill and a great wind picked Aelfric up and blew him deep inside. There, the legend goes, Aelfric still sleeps the sleep of the ages until the end of time. Then he must rise up and give an account of himself.

'It's an interesting legend, and Sir William Fenton became fascinated by it. I think he really believed that Aelfric was sleeping under a hill near the village—a place called Aelfric's Hollow. Sir William started archaeological work there. But though he went back to dig there for many years he never found anything.'

'So is Aelfric there?'

Uncle Alistair laughed. 'Who knows what you'll find when you start looking, Maddy? Aelfric is safely tucked up till the end of time. That's good enough for me. Whether he exists or not is something I don't have to be concerned about.'

'The end of time...' Ralph grew serious. He thought of his dream and the pushing hands. They had seemed to be pushing towards the end of something. A tunnel? But time? Could it have been the end of time? And what lay beyond there—just power—or emptiness—or something else?

'Oh!' Uncle Alistair clapped his hand to his forehead. 'The suitcase!'

Ralph and Maddy gasped—how *could* they have forgotten it?

Uncle Alistair ran upstairs. 'Mind you,' he called down, 'Aelfric might have something to do with all this. There were some funny things in Sir William's book as I recall.'

'Great!' said Maddy. 'An ancient warrior is all we need.'

'He's asleep till the end of time,' said Ralph.

'I know, but people wake up,' said Maddy as they followed Uncle Alistair up to his bedroom.

They watched him take out the boards at the back of the wardrobe and open the safe. The suitcase was still there.

Uncle Alistair relaxed. 'I was ninety-eight per cent sure nobody could get in,' he said, 'but you never know. The burglars got near enough today.' He hauled the case out. 'Funny,' he frowned, shaking it.

Ralph touched it. The gold snakes gleamed coolly up at him. 'It's—there's a kind of humming inside,' he said.

Uncle Alistair swivelled the suitcase and started to open the locks. Ralph and Maddy stepped back.

'But you said we mustn't...' said Ralph, anxiously.

'Oh!' A dull glow illuminated Maddy's face as she jumped back.

'How peculiar!' said Uncle Alistair. 'It's like...'

Ralph couldn't help himself. He stared down into the depths of the case. The black now pricked with shining shapes, distant and throbbing. Far, far away—too far to reach or even imagine.

'It seems to be full of stars,' said Ralph, 'stars that shine but not with light, only far away—yes—that's right—it's filling with black stars.'

'So something's happening.' Uncle Alistair banged the case shut. 'I don't think it's very healthy to look in there too long. But we'll take it downstairs again just to make sure.'

'Stars? Why?' said Maddy. She could not get the thought out of her head. Why should the case fill with black stars?

The early evening sunlight gilded all the leaves of the wood with a golden sheen. Ralph had been sent out to the garden to pick raspberries. Uncle Alistair had a small vegetable and fruit patch there, by the side of the house, and Gail did most of the gardening. Ralph walked among the rows of tall canes. Raspberries in bright, jewelled globules dangled down like miniature chandeliers. Ralph filled his bowl quickly with the ripe berries, his thoughts elsewhere. His hands were stained with sweet juice and his mouth was full. He was humming a tune. That was when he saw the soldier.

The man's metal helmet crowned a stern face. He had a narrow-barrelled musket slung over one shoulder. The soldier stood alone and had an alert, hunted look about him. He opened his mouth to utter words Ralph could not hear, then turned—and walked through the garden wall!

Ralph could not take his eyes from the section of brick wall where the soldier had disappeared. He was convinced that anything—anything or anyone—might come out of the wall towards him now. As he watched, the tingling feeling he had experienced before by the river came over him again. For a moment, time around him stood still. It was as if there was no time, as if 'now' could blow away with the slightest whiff of breeze. The colour, the texture, the material of the wall—even of Ralph himself—seemed to drain and become clear—like glass. It was as if everything had thinned to the flimsiest curtain, which could suddenly be ripped apart. Then the infinite, the beyond—whatever there was at the end of time—would come rushing in to engulf everything.

'Ralph!' There was worry in Uncle Alistair's voice as he approached.

Ralph came back to himself. 'Yes?' He noticed that the bowl of raspberries was only half full.

'Are you all right?'

'I think so. It's just that everything went sort of ... clear ... for a moment.'

'I know,' Uncle Alistair agreed. 'It's happening again. I can feel it too.'

The good thing about Uncle Alistair was that you hardly ever had to explain. He generally accepted what you said, no matter how odd.

'What is it?'

'Time—time growing thin and returning to normal. I have a hunch that someone is trying to sift through time, to the very end of it—and these appearances are the result.'

'The end of ... time ... but what *is* at the very end of time?'

'Who can tell? Something terrible. Something wonderful!'

In the hall, the phone rang. Maddy picked it up, half-afraid. She had hated the sinister click-followed-by-silence when she had answered before.

'Hello?' She spoke carefully.

'Hello!' A warm voice answered. 'Is that Maddy? It's Nick Fleming here.'

'I'll go and get Uncle Alistair for you,' she said. 'Phone!'

she called, running out into the garden. 'It's the phone!'

'For me?'

'Yes.'

'Hello,' said Uncle Alistair, returning.

'Nick here. Glad to have caught you. I know it's late, but I thought I'd better—ah—report. The painting in the schoolhouse is fully uncovered now. I've been hard at work. Would you like to come and have a look at it? Come now—the playgroup's using one of the classrooms all day tomorrow.'

'We'll be right there, if that's all right with you.'

'Oh, yes, yes—I'm free till nine thirty.'

'It's the painting!' There was a barely contained excitement in the way Uncle Alistair spoke. 'Now we're going to see the whole thing!'

Uncle Alistair's expression showed he was impressed. He gazed at the full picture. 'I would never have thought it.'

'It hasn't moved again, anyway,' said Nick with relief.

There were still some pieces of plaster stuck to the painting, but now the whole panel had been unmasked. The third and fourth knights were plainly visible, one riding a chestnut horse, the other riding a red. The knight on the chestnut horse had his face towards the onlookers. His features were stamped with some kind of warning. Beneath the knights the ground knotted in the tendrils of an intertwining pattern which rose to form a mound. The mound dominated the left-hand part of the picture. It was the mound and what was painted inside which were so fascinating.

The mound had a green exterior, but was hollow and white inside. In its heart lay a figure on a stone slab. Around this sleeping figure were scattered black shapes, like stars. The figure was a man with a beard and he was dressed in black. The sleeper's hands were folded over his chest.

'Is that ...' whispered Maddy.

'The Black Warrior—Aelfric!' affirmed Uncle Alistair. 'It must be!'

'You seem remarkably well informed.' Nick sounded respectful. 'I must say, I was surprised to see this. I know the Aelfric legend, but not ...'

'I know, not ... in this connection.'

'That'll knock a few theories on the head!'

'Why?' asked Maddy.

'Well,' said Uncle Alistair, 'Aelfric's the big local legend really. Go to the gift shop in the High Street and you can find all sorts of items with Aelfric on them. The legend of the four horsemen is less well known ... people don't pay so much attention to them. This painting is the first piece of evidence that the four horsemen have any connection with Aelfric. You can see here that the two legends are linked. No one has known that before.'

'What does that mean?' asked Ralph.

'Something important,' said Uncle Alistair, 'that we are going to have to find out!'

5

Maddy drifted through space. She was dreaming she was drenched in darkness—in the infinite black of space. Her feet tilted past asteroids and planets, past meteors with flickering tadpole tails, and past endless fiery suns. She could have drifted for ever—but there was no ever—only space, without beginning and end. In her dream, she wanted to come to the end of everything! That was what she really wanted, *all* she wanted. But she could not.

She did not know how long she had been journeying because time no longer had any meaning for her. As she glided in the impenetrable blackness, she began to turn. Round and slowly round she went, like a leaf on the surface of a sleepy pool. Then faster. Suddenly, she was caught in a whirl, in the midst of an inexplicable current in space. She found herself pulled· like a magnet towards something she could not see and into something— something even blacker than the black of space. It was a black star. Maddy felt the star pulse to swallow her. Her feet and legs and body plunged into its heart and then— she found that it had not been a black star at all, but a kind of hole in the fabric of space.

Maddy fell through it to find herself in Uncle Alistair's back garden. She lay on the grass. The sun was high overhead and there were a few threads of cloud. Around her she heard—she did not know what—a babble of invisible voices. Around her, too, under the grass, from the insides of the trees, from within the wall, came the mighty pushing of hands. There were so many hands and they were all pushing. Pushing. Maddy knelt in a corner of the garden near the base of the wall. She put out her hand and found that the wall was not solid brick any more. She trembled with surprise. It looked like a wall, but there was nothing there—it had been eaten away by something inside that was trying to come out.

Time, the curtain of time, was being pushed by a myriad of invisible fingers. What would happen, what could happen, if that curtain parted? What would be unleashed? She gasped as, without warning, a hand shot through the wall and grabbed her by the wrist. She tried to wrestle free, yelling, 'No! No!' She struggled. Through the wall she saw a forest of hands pushing out towards her. The hands seemed to be formed of solid shadow—dark as night. Maddy screamed.

'Maddy,' came a voice in her dream, 'do not be afraid!' It was Uncle Alistair. He towered behind her, taller than she'd ever seen him before. It was as if he were made of light—a light which came from somewhere else, beyond. Suddenly her heart sang. It was like spring and new life, like the gladness of knowing there's something— someone—beyond everything that will wrap you up and keep you safe and look after you. Wherever the light fell, the dark hands withered and withdrew through the wall.

'Why, they're only shadows!' said Maddy.

'Don't let the darkness deceive you. Know it for what it is!' said Uncle Alistair. 'The darkness will tell you it is all-powerful, that there is no light. But that is a lie! Look!'

The last of the hands flinched at the touch of the light and vanished through the wall.

'You must see and understand, Maddy,' said Uncle Alistair.

Maddy turned around. 'Where does your light come

from?' she asked. 'Can I have some?'

Uncle Alistair laughed. 'It's not *my* light, Maddy,' he said.

In that instant Maddy's mind opened. She *knew* whose light it was. The thought awed her. At the same time it filled her with a wonder so intense that she cried out in joy. She woke up.

That morning Ralph and Maddy had breakfast on their own. Uncle Alistair was busy in his study. He had started work long before they got up. After breakfast he stuck his head out of the study door and called: 'Listen, you two, I really ought to get on with this.'

'What are you doing?' Maddy and Ralph stood in the hall, trying to peer round the door.

'Research!' Uncle Alistair pulled a wry face. 'I'm trying to find out all I can about Aelfric. I might drive in to town to photocopy some of the library's copy of *The Chernton Chronicle*. If Mrs Edwards is at the desk she'll let me use the machine. I could go now. Would you like to come?'

Ralph glanced through the open door and out of the study window. The sun glittered on the river. Light shone on the water like sheer, pure silver. The last thing Ralph wanted to do was go into town. Town meant shops and shops meant shopping. Ralph hated shopping. He had learned that people who seemed normal most of the time—even Maddy—changed as soon as they entered a shop. They wandered round and took ages. They hardly bought anything. Then they became angry if you wanted to hurry up and go somewhere else.

'I'd like to come with you,' said Maddy. 'I ought to buy Mum a present, anyway.'

'Fine! Ralph?'

Ralph squirmed. He never found it easy to step out of line. 'I think,' he said, 'I'll stay here. I may go down to the river.'

'Suit yourself. If you go into the village, mind—leave a note. I don't want to come home and find I don't know where you've got to! Five minutes, Maddy—I've some books to take back to the library, and I've got to find them first!'

Maddy had learned there were times when Ralph preferred to be on his own, and she knew he hated shops.

Ralph's family was a noisy one. The twins were always full of energy and running around. They dominated the house. Ralph's father had pupils come for extra lessons—and Ralph's mother taught the piano and took some evening students for French. The house was always full of busy confusion. It was little wonder that Ralph sometimes vanished—slunk up to his room, the one place in the house which was his, where he could be quiet and close the door on everybody else.

When Maddy and Uncle Alistair had driven off, Ralph wandered through the rooms downstairs, wondering what to do. The river curved beyond the window but he no longer wanted to go there. Ralph stopped. Outside the bay window was a man. Ralph thought his heart would stop beating. It was someone Ralph recognized—Mr Barnes!

Mr Barnes had gone into hospital. He was proud of his greenhouse and grew plants which he sold to the neighbours. Ralph had got into a stone-throwing match and his stones had smashed some panes of the green-house glass. Instead of owning up, Ralph had hidden and blamed the breakage on another boy, a boy who wasn't very bright and could not defend himself. Everyone has a few dark secrets, and this was one of Ralph's. He hadn't thought of it in a long time. Now here was Mr Barnes—

out of time, out of place—at the window. Only it couldn't be Mr Barnes, not *now*, because he wasn't—well, he wasn't alive any more. Ralph began to shake. He looked again. The figure had gone.

'I can't . . . I'm not going to stay in,' shivered Ralph to himself. He hurried into the hall.

He stopped outside Uncle Alistair's study. Then he went in. Books and papers were piled high on one side on Uncle Alistair's messy desk. The insect-like jointed lamp hung over it and was still switched on. A pamphlet entitled SIR WILLIAM AND HIS SEARCH FOR AELFRIC: A LIFETIME'S OBSESSION by HARRIET CRUICKSHANK was propped against a paperweight. Uncle Alistair had scribbled a rough sketch of the wall painting at the schoolhouse on a sheet of paper, showing the positions of the knights and the mound where Aelfric was sleeping.

The painting. Why not go and have a look at that? Maybe the figures had moved again. Maybe they would tell him something. Ralph scribbled a note and left.

'How long will you need to buy your present, Maddy?' Uncle Alistair's eyes scanned the road as he tried to negotiate the roundabout into town. There was always such a jam at this time of morning.

Maddy was sitting beside Uncle Alistair in the front of the car with the seat-belt strapped.

'I don't know. A while.'

'Well, there's no hurry. Take as long as you like. I can drop you off at the shopping centre.'

'Thanks. Oh, just one thing . . .'

'Yes?'

'There is one thing bothering me. Are we—I mean— are we . . . safe?'

Uncle Alistair merely tapped his fingers on the rim of

the steering-wheel as he edged his car into the flow of traffic. He did not answer.

Ralph walked into the village. The heat was even more intense today. It pressed down so that he could hardly think. His eyes were blinded by the glare of the sun.

'Any more of this and we'll fry,' thought Ralph. He wondered, just for a moment, if the heat had anything to do with what was going on, but he put that thought out of his mind.

Seeing Mr Barnes had shaken Ralph. Someone was tampering with time. Past and present were somehow all mixed up. It wasn't the dead Mr Barnes he'd seen. He'd worked that one out now. It was Mr Barnes in the past being brought through to the present. Ralph could not blot out his questions about the end of time. And then there was his dream—it all came back to him now—the hands, the pushing hands. What was their purpose? Not a good one.

Ralph was confused. Usually he just took things for granted. But thinking about the end of time had frightened him. Ralph looked at the trees and the hedgerows. What *did* lie at the end of time? What *was* beyond everything he knew? The end of time had to be the end of everything, everything that was possible, everything that could be imagined. What then? Was there nothing? Or some sort of blind power or, as Uncle Alistair had said, something terrible and wonderful? Did the Light Uncle Alistair had talked about come from the same source?

Then there was the painting. Was it warning them in some way? How could a painting *move*? Uncle Alistair said that in times of dire need higher rules than the ones we normally knew could come into play. Was that what was happening now? It was maddening to see the figures change and yet not understand their meaning.

Ralph arrived at the schoolhouse and gazed up and

down the road. One man was hanging about, but there was no one else. He seemed to be hesitating.

With a jolt Ralph realized it was the fair-haired man they had seen in the village and taken for Sir George. Ralph opened the gate and ran up to the front entrance.

The schoolhouse was open. Photos for the WORLD-WIDE EXHIBITION lay on the floor of the cloakroom ready to be put up. There was a lot of noise coming from the classroom where the playgroup was gathering. Nick and the workmen had not yet arrived.

Ralph went through to the hall. He lifted the sheet to look at the painting. A tingle went through him. The picture had changed again. Now the white horse and its rider had advanced to the left, and the knight on the red horse was facing Ralph. He was holding his sword aloft in warning. On the left-hand side of the picture the black stars round the figure of Aelfric appeared to be crowding closer to him. What were they doing? Why had the artist painted *black* stars in Aelfric's Hollow . . .?

'What are you doing here?'

Ralph jumped. He had not heard anyone approaching. Mrs Williams from the playgroup stood glaring at him.

'Don't you know that Mr Fleming has expressly forbidden anyone to touch the painting? That includes you! Now, off you go. If I catch you here again I'll report you! What's your name, boy?'

If there was one thing Ralph hated even more than shopping it was being called 'boy'.

'Ralph.'

'You're not from the village, are you?'

'I'm staying with my Uncle Alistair—the house past the crossroads.'

'Oh, him!' Mrs Williams gave Ralph a funny look. 'Your uncle, is he? Well, off you go and don't let me catch you looking at that painting again!'

Mrs Williams turned her back on Ralph. With a stately walk she disappeared into the classroom.

'I'll drop you here,' said Uncle Alistair to Maddy. He drew up on a double yellow line outside the glass doors of the new shopping centre. THE MARKET CENTRE was worked in rainbow coloured stones into the pavement outside. 'Forty-five minutes, is that OK? I shouldn't be any longer than that.'

'That's fine,' said Maddy.

'Careful how you open your door.'

Maddy opened her door and got out onto the pavement. She waved. Uncle Alistair tooted and drove on.

Ralph stood on the steps of the schoolhouse. He did not like what he saw. Sir George—if it was Sir George—was walking towards him. He stopped by the wooden gate.

'Good morning,' he said as Ralph came down the path.

'Good morning.'

Ralph made to pass him. As he did so, he noticed something about the man's face. The skin was rough and flaky as if there was hardly any moisture in him. When he spoke, his voice was dry. It came out as a hoarse whisper.

'Have you been looking at the painting?' he asked.

'The painting?'

'There is a painting in there, isn't there? The whole village is talking about its new-found treasure.' The man searched inside his jacket pocket for a cigarette. 'My name's Fenton, by the way. I live at the Grange.' He nodded in the direction of his house.

So it *was* Sir George. 'Why don't you go and look at the painting yourself?' said Ralph.

'It's out of bounds, isn't it?'

For a moment Ralph wondered how Mrs Williams would have tackled Sir George.

'Besides,' Sir George took a grateful puff at his cigarette, 'what would I want to go in *there* for?'

'Well . . .'

'Don't go!' Sir George rattled out the words as Ralph began to walk away. 'Come with me to the Grange. I'm going back for coffee and I'd like to know more about that uncle of yours.'

'How do you . . .'

Sir George laughed again. 'This is a village,' he said. 'News travels fast. I know more than you think.' He stared Ralph straight in the eyes. Sir George's eyes were small and brilliant. They reminded Ralph of a snake. 'Come along with me now,' he said firmly. 'I'll let your uncle know where you are, if that's what's worrying you.'

Ralph swallowed hard. He noticed the buttons on Sir George's jacket. They were gold—two intertwining snakes! The sun caught them, and for a moment Ralph thought he saw the snakes crawl over Sir George's body and hiss at him.

Sir George leant towards Ralph, and the boy was suddenly overwhelmed. To his consternation he found his legs moving in the direction Sir George was pointing. He tried to resist. He tried to say something, but nothing—not his voice, not his legs—would obey him. One step forward and then another, he made his way towards the Grange.

'Thank you for accepting my invitation,' said Sir George coolly. 'I'm sure we are going to have a most interesting time.'

Fortunately for Uncle Alistair Mrs Edwards *had* been on the desk at the library. It was one of her three mornings in. She knew he'd be careful. But the supervisor was about, she told him, and there might be questions. You could damage a fragile book by photocopying it roughly. And the library had its rules.

Uncle Alistair placed *The Chernton Chronicle* on the glass of the photocopier. Flash! That was one page, and he wanted quite a few. This was going to take some time. He wished he had read his own copy of Sir William Fenton's book more thoroughly before it had been stolen. Then he might have some... clue... about why Aelfric was important, if, indeed, he was. And was there some connection with the suitcase?

'Welcome to the Grange!'

Sir George opened the front door and stood back for Ralph to enter. The front of the house was shielded from the village by a screen of beech trees and shrubs, creating the impression that it was out in the country. There was hardly a sound.

Sir George motioned Ralph inside and Ralph's body obeyed. To his dismay, Sir George locked the front door behind him. Heavy furniture crowded the narrow hall. The carpet was a rich chocolate brown with green vine leaves threaded through it. Ralph could hear people moving upstairs, and there seemed to be whispers, disembodied, hanging near the ceiling. Hands pressed faintly from the other side of the mirror as he passed. The piercing shriek of a parrot broke the silence. The frenzied bird hopped on its perch and cracked nuts with its beak.

'Do come in,' invited Sir George. The room Ralph was shown into lay at the back of the house. It had been Sir James' own private sitting-room and his books still lined the shelves in undisturbed rows. A worn leather sofa faced the window.

'I think it's time for a little talk,' Sir George began.

Ralph felt his whole body go ice-cold in the grip of grasping, invisible fingers. Sir George sat down in an armchair opposite Ralph. There was a mahogany table between them. A single book lay on it. Ralph's eyes strayed to the title: *The Chernton Chronicle* by Sir William Fenton. A smile spread over Sir George's face. Beside the book rested something circular made out of brass. Ralph guessed it was a kind of badge or ornament. It was of two intertwining snakes in a circle.

'So!' Sir George seemed satisfied. 'I have been put to quite a bit of trouble since you arrived. Now, maybe you can help me.'

Uncle Alistair finished his photocopying. The paper from the machine was still warm. He was about to shut the book when he decided to have a look at the preface. He had skipped that before. Mrs Edwards came in.

'Haven't you finished yet? I need to get on that machine. If the supervisor comes in and finds I've let you copy that precious book I'll be for it!'

'Just a minute... there may be something here I've missed. I don't think I've ever read the preface before.'

Uncle Alistair read as fast as he could. What was this? He came to 'at which time I did most earnestly determine to seek out the truth of this wondrous legend. For if it be true that there are powers in this world we little dream of, why should they not lie sleeping beneath our feet? Why should they not be awakened? Thus I began my long study.'

'This seems intriguing... I'll have to copy this, Margaret.' Uncle Alistair frowned. 'Just give me a minute, will you? If the supervisor comes—stall her!'

'I'll do my best!' Mrs Edwards laughed. 'But if she walks in and sees you, then you'll be the one with the explaining to do! Is that a deal?'

'It's a deal,' agreed Uncle Alistair.

'You must talk to me,' said Sir George. 'There is so little pleasure in a silent guest.'

Ralph felt the muscles round his throat relax. Sir George sat facing him. The man's dry features were concentrated and eager. His fair, boyish eyebrows were almost invisible under his peeling brow. His eyes were wells of fathomless dark.

'We have a little project here, you might say. It's very important that it succeeds. We're fitting pieces together— like a jigsaw. Only, one of the pieces has gone missing. It's a very important piece, perhaps the *most* important piece. We can probably manage without it, but if we had it—then we would be certain to accomplish our task!'

Sir George's hand tightened into a rock-hard fist.

'What kind of project?' asked Ralph. His hands were getting cold.

'It was begun last century by my great-great-grandfather, Sir William Fenton. He used to live here at the Grange. That's a portrait of him by the door. He was dismissed in his day as a crank, a buffoon! But he knew he had stumbled across something significant, something other people never could, never would notice—though it lay under their noses. Sir William dedicated his life to one passion—and in the end it killed him. Now his passion has become mine, and I intend to see his work completed!'

'What work? What are you talking about? Why ... why can't I ... I want to go home!'

'I will not be stopped!' Sir George's eyes blazed. For a moment, from within they revealed something dark, formless and terrifying. He smiled again and the impression passed.

'I believe you can help me. Perhaps we can help each

other. Wouldn't you like to have anything you want—
everything you have ever wanted? It could all come to
you with a snap of your fingers. You can't stop me, but
you can help me! I am on the verge of a tremendous
discovery, you see—something which could change . . .
everything . . . for ever . . .!' Sir George's eyes glittered.

'I . . .' Ralph gasped. He repeated the words with
difficulty. 'I want to go!'

'Don't you understand? Don't you understand at all? I
am talking about the key—the key!' Sir George stood up
and began to pace around the room. 'I am talking about
the one thing which no one can withstand!' He turned to
Ralph. 'I am talking about power!'

6

'Power!' Sir George's features lit up with expectant triumph. 'Power!' The word carried round the room. 'Imagine—the power to do anything! Anything! Beside me, an ordinary man will soon be as feeble as an insect!'

Sir George's expression softened to a dreaminess which broke as he swung his attention back to Ralph.

'So, you see, this little project of mine is too important to let anyone—*anyone*—stand in the way. My friends have travelled long distances to come here. Some have—er—paid a price to do so, you might say. They are not to be deterred! What we are about is nothing less than the birth of a new era! All that has gone before, all the failures of history, will be swept away! Then we will be kings—conquerors!'

Sir George wiped the spittle from his bloodless lips. As he did so, Ralph noticed something happening to the window behind his captor. The panes started to twist as if buckling under some pressure. A thin mist fanned up from the old radiator. The glass whitened and became opaque.

Ralph watched, fear branching inside him. Before, he had been able to gaze out at the flower-beds and beech trees and had felt—well, in touch with reality—that he would probably be able to stand up and walk out when Sir George had finished with him. Now he was not so sure. As the garden disappeared behind the veil of milky mist,

Ralph felt his throat go dry. He was afraid. He did not know what to do.

'In you get, Maddy!' Uncle Alistair leaned across the passenger seat and opened the car door for her. 'I'm sorry to have kept you waiting, but I had more to photocopy than I thought.'

'That's all right. I sat and watched the jugglers.'

Uncle Alistair headed away from the shopping centre towards the road which led to Lower Chernton.

'What did you get for your mother, then?'

Maddy had a wrapped square box on her lap.

'One of those plants in a box. Mum likes plants, you see. Our house is full of them.'

'I like plants too.' Uncle Alistair wound down his window to let in some air. 'Though I never seem to find the time to water them.'

'What did you find out?'

Uncle Alistair patted the manila envelope at his side. 'A lot, I think. Sir William Fenton was on to Aelfric, that's for sure. He thought that if he dug Aelfric up he could awaken him. He believed Aelfric's Hollow was somehow "out of time" and that Aelfric himself was a link to the "end of time". I'm not sure how sensible all this is, or how true. Sir William believed that at the end of time lay a great power, there for the taking. He believed he was the only person who recognized this.'

'Perhaps he was—then,' replied Maddy.

'Yes, well, I don't know everything yet, because I haven't read through all the material. Sir William copied down some interesting symbols, though—the black star for one. It's a mark of power, according to him—but it can also be a hole or a kind of tunnel through to the end of time.'

'The suitcase!' breathed Maddy.

'You're quick,' said Uncle Alistair. 'It's no wonder they want it. They must think it's their way to Aelfric and unlimited power, but . . .'

'But what?'

'Let me put it this way. Greed blinds people. And power can make people believe they can do anything. That's not a good combination. What if Sir William was tampering with something he really didn't understand? The world may not have been made the way he thought it was. The rules may be written so deep that they are beyond the understanding of power-blinded people like Sir William and Sir George.'

'Rules—what rules?'

'The rules of how things are and how they are meant to be. Finding out how things are is important. It involves understanding as well as seeing. Sir George and his friends are scrabbling about in the dark—and that's dangerous because there *is* power involved. If you're in the dark what you really need is light. But Sir George and his friends don't like the light much. They'd rather go their own way and get what they can.'

Back at the house, Uncle Alistair walked briskly up the front steps and opened the door into the hall.

'Ralph! Ralph!' he cried. 'We're back!' But there was no answer. The house was empty.

'Where did he say he was going, Maddy?'

'Down by the river.'

Uncle Alistair strode into the living-room and stared through the bay window. His eyes searched the riverbank.

'No, he's not down there.'

'Oh, here!' Maddy picked up Ralph's note from the table. 'He's gone to the schoolhouse to look at the painting.'

'Look at the painting—on his own? *Not* a good idea!'

'Why not?'

'You looked in the suitcase on your own, didn't you—and look what happened! I wonder when he went.'

'I don't know. He hasn't written a time.'

'We'll have to wait, then. Honestly, I do wish people would try and be sensible!'

'Power!' Sir George's mouth gaped like a deep, dark cave. 'Power is might and might is good! The old ideas of right and wrong are only for the weak. But for some of us power is a birthright. We are fated to it. Not the power of armies or politicians—the power to change and shape the world. Those born to this power must reach up to the stars and seize their destiny. They are emperors in disguise. But the time is coming when we will throw off the disguise and reveal ourselves to the world. We shall sweep everything before us! We shall consume like fire! It is in this village that the secret lies. That is why we have gathered here. Soon the last will arrive and then— tonight, tomorrow—when our numbers are complete, we shall begin!'

'Begin what?'

Sir George smiled, his face mask-like. He let out a roar of harsh laughter.

'Our journey to the end of time!'

'Ralph isn't back yet,' said Maddy. Two hours had passed since they had arrived home.

She stood at Uncle Alistair's study door, which was open only a crack. She had been afraid to go and disturb him.

Uncle Alistair turned from his desk. 'What is the ... oh, is it that time already? Nearly lunchtime. Ralph should have been back ages ago if he only went to look at the picture.'

'He might have gone into the village afterwards.'

'I thought he didn't like shops. And there's not much else to look at in the village.'

'There are trains. He likes trains. He might have gone down to the station.'

'You're right—once he starts on trains you can never get him away. Shall we go and fetch him? Let's take the car. It'll be quicker. We'll try the schoolhouse first.'

Uncle Alistair stacked his papers neatly and switched off the desk lamp. Five minutes later, he and Maddy turned out of the drive and drove the short distance to the schoolhouse.

'You wait here,' Uncle Alistair said. 'I'll only be a minute.' Maddy watched through the windscreen. Uncle Alistair strode up to the entrance of the schoolhouse. On the other side of the road was the Grange. She could just see the honey-coloured stone of the house through the trees. Maddy's thoughts focused on the secluded house. It looked like any other big house. Quite innocent. But it wasn't. She knew it wasn't. She wondered what was going on in there.

Uncle Alistair peered into the schoolhouse. The workmen were standing by the scaffolding, chatting. Nick Fleming was nowhere to be seen. He knocked on the classroom door where the playgroup was meeting. Mrs Williams answered.

'Good morning!' said Uncle Alistair brightly.

'Oh, hello!' Mrs Williams stepped into the cloakroom. 'I didn't realize you were back.'

'You haven't seen my nephew, have you?'

'I most certainly have!'

Uncle Alistair relaxed with relief. 'Oh, good! Where is he?'

Mrs Williams was frosty. 'I don't known where he is *now*, but he *was* in here earlier. He was looking at the painting.'

'Yes, yes...'

'I am not in the habit of telling other people's children off, but really, Mr Fleming put up a very firm notice and...'

'Thank you, Mrs Williams, I'll have a word with Ralph.'

Mrs Williams scowled at Uncle Alistair. But she did not press the matter. Long ago, she and her husband had wanted to buy the house Uncle Alistair now lived in. She had never really forgiven him for getting to it first.

'Do you have any idea where he's gone?'

'I saw him leave and that was that.'

'Oh, well, I'm sure he'll be in the village somewhere.'

Uncle Alistair attempted a friendly smile. Then he left the schoolhouse and plumped back into the car beside Maddy.

'Well?' she mumbled. She had found a packet of fruit drops in the car.

'No luck. He *was* there, but he isn't there now. It was Mrs Williams who told me. If I was in the playgroup I think I'd have buried her in the sandpit long ago!' The engine revved. 'Let's try the station.'

Sir George circled the room like a hungry bird of prey.

'I need your help,' he said finally.

'How can I help you?'

A strange sense of coldness was creeping through Ralph. It travelled from his hands up into his arms. His feet felt like solid blocks of ice.

'Because I have lost something. Or rather, it was— mislaid. I think you know what and where it is. You and the girl were at the station the day it should have been delivered.'

Ralph's fear increased. He used all the strength he had left not to mention the suitcase. The daylight in the room was gloomy since the high, square-paned window had misted over. A cloudy web of shadow seemed to cover the furniture and deeper shadows oozed like ink in the corners of the room.

'I think you know what I am talking about!' Sir George's voice was cutting, like a polished blade. 'You see, I don't know *how* it came. I don't know what form it took. All I know is that it came off the train you arrived on. Only the messenger went back on his word. He was frightened, and he ran. Well, we tracked him, we pinned him down. And we made him squeal. All we got out of him pointed to a boy and a girl in the same railway compartment. He had the idea they could somehow neutralize the power of the thing he was carrying. You are the boy, aren't you? And I have seen the girl. No other boy and girl got off that train together. I imagine you know what I am talking about and where it is, don't you? Just give it to me, then—as we say—we can . . . strike a deal.'

Ralph kept his mouth shut and tried to distract himself from the man's accusations.

'Stubborn, I see!' Sir George said quietly. 'Well, if you won't tell *me*, perhaps you'll tell *us*.'

He walked over to the door, picked up a brass handbell and rang it. Its jangle clanged and filled the house.

The railway station was deserted. Maddy and Uncle Alistair walked past the rows of silent cars in the car park. There was no one about.

'We can go in and ask,' said Maddy.

'You can,' said Uncle Alistair. 'I'll have a look round. This isn't like Ralph. He's usually so reliable. I don't think he's here.'

They walked into the ticket office. Uncle Alistair went

out onto the platform to see if Ralph was there. Ralph often sat on one of the station benches when he went to watch trains. Maddy stood by the ticket office. The stationmaster and the ticket man were talking. They didn't see her.

'. . . it was no ghost!' repeated the stationmaster. 'It was as solid as you or me! She just walked through the door!'

'The wife said she saw somebody go up the stairs the other night!' replied the ticket man. 'Makes you think, doesn't it? There's something funny going on.'

'It's worse than that. The woman I saw—I knew her.'

'Knew her!'

'Mona Richardson her name was. I met her—oh—forty years ago. We were going to get married and I backed out. She was terribly cut up, but I—well, I wasn't ready for marriage then. I was too young. I tell you, I never hurt anyone as much as I hurt her. When I saw her staring at me the other night it gave me a turn, I can tell you. I don't even know if she's still alive, but there she was—a bit of my past in the present, and large as life.'

'What did you do?'

'I didn't do anything. I wanted to say sorry, like, for what I'd done to her all those years ago—to try and put right what happened. But she vanished before I had a chance to speak to her. I was too terrified, but I'll tell her if she comes again. I've decided that. She deserves it.'

The stationmaster suddenly became aware that Maddy was standing behind him.

'Now, young lady,' he said, 'what can I do for you?'

'I'm looking for my friend Ralph,' she said. 'He's about the same age as me with sandy hair and jeans. I think he's wearing a red T-shirt.'

The stationmaster looked inquiringly at the ticket man.

'No, sorry, there's been no one like that here this morning. Can't help, I'm afraid.'

Maddy backed away disappointed, with a quiet 'thank you'. As she turned to look for Uncle Alistair, she saw, through the shimmering glass doors of the railway station, Sir George's large black car gliding down the hill into the station car park.

'That'll be for the Reading train,' said the stationmaster. 'I'd better go and see to it.'

'Some more of His Nibs' friends, most likely,' replied the ticket man.

'I know—give you the creeps, don't they?' said the stationmaster, hurrying out.

Maddy ran onto the platform. Uncle Alistair was resting on one of the benches with his legs stretched out and his eyes closed.

'Uncle Alistair! Uncle Alistair!'

'What? Hmmm!' Uncle Alistair opened his eyes slowly and blinked. 'Oh, I'm sorry, Maddy, I was just trying to think where Ralph could be.'

The train snaked round the bend into the station.

'Sir George's car is here.'

'Really? Well, we came at the right time, didn't we?'

Uncle Alistair and Maddy sat on the bench and watched the passengers get off the train—an elderly couple, a businessman and a father with three children. Nothing odd about them. But there were others who drew their attention: a young man with a lion's mane of frizzy hair; two thin, dark strangers; a stout man carrying a box, and a woman in a clinging, black dress. It wasn't so much how they looked or what they wore which marked them out— more an aura, a pre-occupation, a sense of something behind the mask. And the way they drew together—as if they were pulled by a magnet.

The group gathered by Sir George's driver who had

come to meet them—then walked through the station building and out to the car park and Sir George's car.

'Oh, dear!' said Uncle Alistair glumly, 'they look like bad news!'

'So where's Ralph?' asked Maddy.

Uncle Alistair shrugged. 'I don't know. I'm worried now. He's been away too long. Let's drive back through the village. I'll go slowly. You look for him.'

'Wouldn't it be a fine thing,' speculated Sir George, 'if we could possess time instead of letting time possess us? We could live for ever! Imagine parting the curtain of time which keeps everything in its place . . . and stepping through. We would be masters, then, of destiny. What power would be ours!'

Ralph heard the sound of stairs creaking, and people coming down the staircase to the narrow hall outside the door. They were gathering—whoever they were—in answer to Sir George's bell.

'And you will help us,' Sir George went on. 'There is something we should like you to give us.'

Sir George pushed his face close to Ralph's. His breath was warm and sour and sharp. Behind him, the door to the sitting-room yawned wide and Sir George's friends entered. The woman with long hair and the man Ralph and Maddy had seen in the village came in, followed by three men, two young, one middle-aged.

Maddy and Uncle Alistair drove the length of the High Street.

'He isn't here,' said Maddy, peering out of the car window. 'No sign of him.'

'No,' Uncle Alistair said grimly. 'We'd better get home. I don't like this. But there's no point in wandering round and round. For all we know Ralph might be sitting there waiting for us.'

'He might.' But Maddy knew—or sensed—that he wouldn't be.

The animal scents of the people in Sir George's sitting-room were oppressive and powerful. Perfumes and heat and mysterious oils combined to suggest jungles and deserts and the hot darkness that wells up out of rifts in the earth's crust. Ralph's breath grew heavy and irregular again. He could do nothing.

'What do you think we want?' Sir George took Ralph by the chin.

A slow murmur travelled round the semi-circle of figures assembled in front of him by the sofa.

'*Where* is it?' Sir George shook Ralph's head in his grip. 'Just tell us where it is.'

The woman began to laugh. The middle-aged man glanced at the man in dark glasses standing next to him. He did not seem wholly sure what was going on—or if he approved.

'What ... what ...' Ralph heard his voice in the form of a gargle in his windpipe. He could not speak. Unbearable ice had splintered into him and seemed to be concentrating in a block in his middle.

Ralph's head was thrust upwards. Sir George's pitiless fingers left icy imprints which shot into his head and gathered above his eyebrows. His head swirled and he thought it would explode. Ralph sagged forward.

'I shall get an answer!' cried Sir George, as the people around Ralph lunged towards him. Ralph's left arm was grabbed and held outstretched.

Through the drunken swim of his eyes, Ralph saw Sir George point at the twin brass snakes next to the copy of *The Chernton Chronicle* on the table. Did he imagine it, or did the snakes begin to flow and shift? They circled in a slither in and out of each other. One of the creatures opened its mouth and hissed. A clear eye showed through the brass. It wound in a knot and veered away from its partner, wrapping its head and upper body in slender coils round Ralph's outstretched wrist.

Ralph could not move. His whole body was locked as though encased in ice. The snake opened its mouth and rose to strike. Ralph felt the sharp stab of its fangs enter the veins of his wrist. A warm throbbing sped up his arm. When it reached his head, waves of sleep lapped around him. The people and shapes swam, dissolving and breaking into fragments. They disintegrated into dust. He heard distant laughter. With a long sigh which felt as though he were falling into a deep, bottomless pit, Ralph lost consciousness.

The phone rang. Uncle Alistair leapt up to answer it.

'Oh, hello, Valerie!' It was Ralph's mother, ringing to see how Ralph was.

'Yes, yes, we've been out doing all kinds of things. No, no bother! No, Ralph's not here now. He's in the village, I think. Well, when I say "I think" I mean he went out and he's not back yet. Uncle Alistair swallowed, and tapped a nervous foot on the carpet. 'Yes, I'll get him to ring you this evening. No, fine, fine—do I sound jumpy? No, there's no reason. I'll tell Ralph, yes.'

Uncle Alistair shrugged at Maddy who had come out into the hall.

'No, no, Valerie,' Uncle Alistair wound the phone cord round his hand as he spoke, 'no, everything's fine! Just fine!'

7

Maddy sat in the kitchen listening to Uncle Alistair pace up and down in his study. The sun's light slanted onto the table giving a gleam to the glasses on the red-checked cloth. It was hot in the kitchen. But even hotter outside. Ralph—where was he? Maddy could not stop thinking about Ralph. Where *was* he? What was happening in the village? Underneath the ordinary everyday chatter there was anxiety. Fear. And then there was the heat ...

'Maddy?' Uncle Alistair appeared at the door. He stood with his hand on the doorknob.

'Oh!' Maddy jumped.

'Sorry, I surprised you.' Uncle Alistair was brisk. 'But I think we should go out and look for Ralph again. I'd feel better if we did *something*.'

'I don't want to sit here anyway.'

'Good, let's go for another scout round. For all we know, Ralph may be quite all right. But don't be scared. Remember the Light.'

Maddy's thoughts went back to her dream—Uncle Alistair and the Light; the awe and the gladness; the certainty that Someone had her safe. As she left the house she felt strangely comforted.

Ralph felt himself borne up by pillars of smoky, shadowy arms. Blurred presences moved like ghosts. Their words tumbled to him as though he were lodged at the foot of a bottomless well.

'Soon we shall know...'

'Soon we shall raise from the hidden place...'

'Soon the hour will come when there are hours no longer. We shall proclaim the End of Time!'

The muffled shadows twined in and out of each other until Ralph could not tell which was which. They circled until they seemed to complete a gigantic geometric form in space with a hard ball of black at its centre. Then the forms closed in to burst this blackness into dark flame.

Space wrinkled like a cloth in Ralph's head. It was made of silk which crumpled the stars together. The planets, dizzy in their orbits, were eased out of their aeon-long paths. Suns grew cold. A cavern of earth and stone grew over Ralph's head, like ice, and he found himself in the roots of a mountain. And as mountains can dam streams and trap them, so this mountain had trapped stars. But the stars were black as pitch, and they whizzed and buzzed like hornets.

To fall into the depths of one of those stars, Ralph knew, would be to fall into nothing. You would never come out—or perhaps you *would* come out, but in a place so different you could never find your way back. Time lapped backwards and forwards in those stars and their packed energy could set the universe ablaze. Ralph spun in a blackness made blacker by the stars. He spun. He had no eyes, no head, no hands, no body. He spun. He spun and spread into the airless space around him. Ralph's head, his thoughts, grew thin like distant summer cloud. They slipped away to nothing. He breathed. Now he knew nothing, nothing. He was unconscious, wound in a timeless sleep.

Maddy felt tired, so tired. And frightened again now. When they got to the centre of the village, all she wanted to do was sit down.

There were a lot of visitors in the village today. The heat beat down. It was so hot.

'Where do we start?' asked Maddy, with a sigh.

'With a drink, I think,' said Uncle Alistair. 'This heat's making me thirsty. Sit here, Maddy. I'll get you one from the shop.'

While Maddy waited on the bench outside the shop, she began to listen to two young mothers who were waiting to cross the road with pushchairs.

'It's the same all over,' one was saying. She spoke to the other whose toddler was fast asleep. 'It's as if the whole village has become—peopled with the past. I'm afraid to go to sleep at nights! I thought my husband was having me on, but when I came home there was ... well ... an old woman standing there in the living-room. What was I to think! I'm mad, I thought, and if I'm not, then I'm certainly not going to tell anyone else about this! But, after that, I began to ... hear things.'

'Janice,' said the other woman, 'there is something I must tell you. It'll sound weird ... but ... I was in bed one night and I heard a noise like a fire.

'Then something else happened. I don't know if I was dreaming. But I was weeding the garden. Robert was at work and suddenly I saw her—Robert's mother. She died of cancer, you know, a few years ago. She never liked me and I never liked her. After she died I thought—I never really gave her a chance. All the things I could have said came into my head, but I couldn't do anything about it. And then, as I say, I saw her—not a ghost, and not sick at all: as real as you are.

I was so shocked I could hardly speak. I didn't know if this *was* her or some bit of the past shaken up in front of me. I spoke to her then and said I was sorry—how much I'd have liked things to have been better between us.'

'And what happened?'

'She never spoke a word, but I knew she'd understood. Then I bawled my eyes out! But since—I feel kind of ... free. It's like a weight has lifted from me. I told Robert. I don't think he believes me, but he says I'm different. I'm like a new person!'

The other woman went very quiet.

'What's the matter?'

'That happened to me too ... from *my* past. Someone who's still alive. But ...'

'But what?'

'I ought to do what you did and try and put things right ...' The woman's voice faded.

'Everybody's been seeing things,' she said. 'They might be keeping quiet, but I'm positive the whole village knows it's going on.'

The two women set off across the road, still talking. Uncle Alistair returned with two cans of drink.

Just as they were finishing, Sir George's black car drove past them up the High Street, heading for the Grange.

At the sight of it Maddy went cold with fear. She *knew*, she *knew* where Ralph was. She turned to Uncle Alistair.

'It's them!' muttered Uncle Alistair aghast. 'They've got him! And they want the case ...'

Uncle Alistair watched as the car disappeared round the corner.

'We have to go home!' he said. 'We have to go home right away!'

By the time they got back to Uncle Alistair's house, Maddy thought she was going to faint with the heat. But when Uncle Alistair put his hand on the top bar of the gate, she went cold again.

'What's wrong?' she asked.

'Somebody's been here, I know it. Whoever it was

didn't get further than the gate: they've not been in. But I know, I can feel it. Somebody's been pushing, but they haven't got in.'

'Who was it, do you think?'

'One of Sir George's men, most likely. These people are determined all right. They want the case at all costs. We have to be ready, Maddy. We have to be ready for whatever happens. I'm sure they'll try again!'

It grew dark and there was still no sign of Ralph. Uncle Alistair was grim; Maddy was frantic. Ralph had been away the whole day.

'Are you sure there's nothing you can do?'

'What do you expect me to do? asked Uncle Alistair.

'Well ... find Ralph.'

'Like that?' Uncle Alistair snapped his fingers. 'As if by magic?'

Maddy's face fell.

'I'm not a magician, Maddy. I can't conjure Ralph out of thin air. And I certainly can't walk up to Sir George at the Grange and ask for him back.'

'But you *do* things. You do things other people can't.'

'I do things other people *don't* do because they don't realize they *can* do them. That's quite a different thing. The power I have isn't mine. It comes from the Light— because I *ask*. Besides, any kind of power has to be used properly. Otherwise, instead of doing the good you want to do, you may end up doing harm.'

'But I'm sure Ralph's there ...' said Maddy. 'Isn't there *anything* you can do?'

'Believe me,' said Uncle Alistair, 'if there were any way I could bring him here I would.'

Maddy walked towards the bay window. The blackness of the night pressed against the glass. The countryside was invisible now. Maddy wondered what was happening to Ralph. She shuddered to think of him penned up by Sir George and his friends.

Flop. Something soft landed on the window. It fixed on one of the panes.

'What's that?' thought Maddy.

Flop. Another landed. Maddy tried to make out its shape. It was something dark, something living. Flop. Maddy saw fingers and the shape of a hand. Flop. Half a dozen shadow hands were pawing at the window, fingers scratching at the glass. Maddy screamed.

'Maddy, what is it?'

'At the window—there are—things at the window.'

Uncle Alistair took Maddy by the shoulders. 'I was expecting *something* nasty,' he said, 'but not that.'

The hands were at all the windows and on the roof of the house. Beyond, by the trees, Uncle Alistair sensed shadows rising ready to encircle the house and close in.

Just then, all the lights went out. Maddy stifled a scream.

'Matches, Maddy!'

'What ... what?' Maddy rubbed the tears out of her eyes.

'Matches—to counter darkness we need light! Here— you do the downstairs, I'll do the upstairs! Now hurry!'

Uncle Alistair lit a candle on the table in front of them.

'But ... but ...'

She heard the soft pat of more shadows landing on the window.

Maddy's hand shook, but she seized the candle and ran round the room lighting all the others from it. She dashed out into the hall to light the candles there and the two in Uncle Alistair's study. She went into the kitchen. Hands heaved at the window.

'They're coming in! They're coming in!' yelled Maddy. 'Uncle Alistair!'

Uncle Alistair's feet pounded on the stair.

'Light the candles! Quick, Maddy!'

Maddy lit a candle and held it up as Uncle Alistair appeared beside her. He took the candle from her and set it close to the glass. The hands drew back.

'What is it? What is happening?'

'Sir George has sent a few messengers to get the case back. They can't defeat the light.'

Maddy followed Uncle Alistair back into the living-room. The black against the windows was now the black of hundreds of shadows, all seeking their prey.

The candles burned. Where their light fell the shadows melted and vanished. There was something more than candle-power here, something old and deep that went back to the beginning of the world.

Maddy watched the points of living flame. There was something so tremendous in the light that you felt very small beside it. The flame was pure and dissolved the darkness. It was alive, like a heart, like life, like hope. And Maddy sensed the pain as well as the power in the flame—it was wounded as well as triumphant. The sheer goodness of the flame, the life of the light, beckoned her, was ready to welcome her.

'You see, don't you,' said Uncle Alistair, 'the Light invites—it does not compel. Because its power comes out of suffering and is used with understanding.'

'But they're *candles*!' said Maddy.

'What did I tell you before?' said Uncle Alistair. 'The candles represent—they *show*—what's really happening. And that's something we can't usually see: the Light is greater than all the powers of darkness.'

Steadily the candles burned. Slowly they turned back the tide of darkness. The shadows retreated. Light swallowed the darkness, as if the shadows had never been.

'The light shines in the darkness,' said Uncle Alistair,

'but the darkness has not overcome it!'

'But why does the light hurt?' asked Maddy.

'Your eyes, you mean? Why don't you shade them?'

'No, the *light* hurts—it's in pain.'

'You can see that, can you? How should I put it? Do you know what sacrifice is—when one thing is offered in place of another? Maddy, once there was a sacrifice offered in place of all others. That sacrifice was willing, but painful, and it brought the light flooding into the world. That's why the light hurts—it was wounded. It won its power through pain. I hope and trust that this same light burns in me. It is beautiful—but it can be terrible too.' Uncle Alistair stood up. 'I think they're going now—what's left of them.'

Maddy stared. The tide of shadow round the house was ebbing.

'Now is the time,' said Uncle Alistair picking up a candle, 'now, while they are retreating through an open door. I shall send a message out with the light. Ralph! Ralph! Hear me!'

Uncle Alistair's words crashed against the walls and the whole house seemed to shudder.

'There, Maddy, we'll see if that will do any good!'

8

Somewhere, a gathering in the darkness began, a gathering back to a faint point of consciousness.

Ralph!

He was Ralph again, dizzy, who-knew-where? But Ralph. Arms of light encircled him and he smelled the perfume of fresh leaves against his face.

Uncle Alistair's voice calling him sent his blood coursing. His uncle's voice pounded in his body like spring, like the voice of spring calling plants to new life. He was rising, rising as though breaking the surface of the water after a long dive.

Ralph lay with night coolness caressing his face. He rolled onto his side. The ground was hard beneath him. He explored his surroundings with his palms, with his eyes still shut.

Ralph felt calm. He opened his eyes. Stars hung above him and blinked through the arms of the trees. He was outside somewhere. *He was outside.*

The strength had gone from his legs but he pulled them into his chest and sat up. He tried to stand. His wrist throbbed cold, so that the whole hand including the fingers was numb. The leaves whispered and the sounds of the wood carried through the still, night air.

As Ralph stood, he tried to take his bearings. A gate! His hands grasped it. The gate was familiar! He was... he was at the end of Uncle Alistair's drive! But how? Unfastening the gate he stumbled towards the welcoming lights of the house.

The bell rang. It jarred the silence of the hall. Uncle Alistair and Maddy were sitting in the living-room. The shadows had finally gone.

'Who's that now?' said Uncle Alistair, getting up wearily.

He opened the door and Ralph staggered in. He lurched and fell sprawling across the threshold.

'Ralph! Ralph! How on earth ...?'

'I ... I ...' the words gargled out of Ralph's mouth. The boy's eyes closed and he fainted.

'So that's it!' Uncle Alistair sat intently in the armchair next to the fireplace, stroking his chin with his hand. 'Power!'

Ralph lay on the sofa wrapped in one of Granny's Scottish blankets.

'Yes—power ... and time. Sir George kept going on about those. I don't know—something about us possessing time instead of letting time possess us. And something about the end of time, too.'

'Tch!' Uncle Alistair waved his hand as though he did not care to listen. 'These people are playing a dangerous game!'

Maddy came in with three cups of cocoa. Ralph sat up to take one, but held his left arm to his side.

'What's wrong?' Uncle Alistair was quick.

'Something—something funny happened at the Grange.' Ralph sounded confused. 'There were these snakes, but metal ones—then ... one of them bit me.'

'Show me.'

Uncle Alistair leaned over the sofa and took Ralph's arm. Ralph's wrist had been punctured by two ugly black spots. The skin around them was puckered blue and purple. Ralph's hand was cold to Uncle Alistair's touch and the frozen whiteness seemed to have spread almost to the elbow.

'They *are* nasty bites.' Uncle Alistair shook his head. 'This will hurt, now. Are you ready for it?'

Ralph nodded. Uncle Alistair took a firm hold of Ralph's arm. The warmth of his touch battled against the cold in Ralph's veins. He lifted Ralph's arm and laid two fingers across the bite marks. Ralph yelped, as though bitten again. Hot pain shot from Uncle Alistair's fingers up towards the shoulder.

'That hurt!' said Ralph.

'The feeling will come back slowly. It will heal. But, really, that was a horrible thing to do. If that bite hadn't been treated...'

'I think Sir George likes showing off his powers,' said Ralph, 'at least, in front of all those people. His friends.'

'People like Sir George don't have friends. Power like his doesn't create friendship, it creates fear,' said Uncle Alistair, grimly.

'But...' Ralph saw, however, that his uncle had not finished.

'From what you say, I think Sir George has chosen a dark road. You see, all of us have power of one kind or another. Just to live, to be alive, is to have power. But how to use that power, that's the test! Power must be matched by love. On its own, power eats away its user until only a shell is left. Those who seek power alone—for its own sake—often end up destroying themselves. The pity is that they can take so many others with them. But power with love is different—it obeys different rules. It is exercised in the light!'

'Why did they let Ralph go?' Maddy asked as she crept round the sofa.

'Because...' Uncle Alistair thought carefully before he

answered. 'Because they thought I couldn't cure the bite. And they knew that if the poison had worked its way through Ralph's system they would have him in their power. Anyway, they knew that in the end I would have called the police and sent them to the Grange in a routine search. That might have uncovered something Sir George didn't want others to see. And because . . .'

'Yes?' Maddy was listening hard.

'Because the people at the Grange want the case.'

'Only, Sir George doesn't know it's a case,' said Ralph suddenly.

'Really?'

'No, Sir George knew *something* was going to come off that train, but he didn't know what it was going to look like.'

'But Sir George knows we have "it"—whatever "it" is,' said Uncle Alistair. 'And of course he thought that Ralph would have delivered it back to him.'

'Sir George said that they could manage without it,' said Ralph. 'But he didn't say what they were going to manage. Tonight and tomorrow, he said.'

'I can guess what they'll try to do,' said Uncle Alistair.

'What's that?'

'Wake up Aelfric. That's what I found out today while you were at the Grange. Sir George believes there's power at the end of time and that Aelfric's going to help him get it.'

'But that's mad!' said Ralph.

'It's what they're going to do, anyway.'

'So that's why all those people have come to the Grange.'

'What about the appearances?' asked Maddy. 'How do they fit in?'

'I told you before. They're bits of the past—bits of history—knocked off and floating free. Like echoes.'

99

'Not just history,' Maddy said. 'People are seeing people they know. I heard that in the village today.'

'I . . . I saw someone this morning,' said Ralph. 'That's why I went out.'

'Really?'

'Yes,' said Maddy, 'I heard one woman say that she said sorry to her mother-in-law or something and then the mother-in-law went away.'

'Who did you see, Ralph?'

Ralph felt his uncle's eyes on him. He gulped. 'Someone I should have said sorry to.'

'How fascinating.'

'Why?' Maddy asked Uncle Alistair.

'Well, at first the appearances were purely historical— but now it's as though bits of people's own pasts are being shaken out of them—the bits that need putting right. Sometimes, you see, what at first seems like a threat is really an opportunity.'

'But why is it happening?'

'Because of the disturbances in time. Only, I told you, time is an experience as much as anything else. The disturbance has caused people to conjure up parts of their own past which, in a way, they need to confront. The village might look sleepy but there must be a lot of people having sleepless nights this week. Which reminds me, I'm tired and I think Ralph needs a good night's sleep. It's about time we all turned in. Agreed?' Uncle Alistair yawned. 'Today has been quite long enough for me.'

But they sat on in silence, too tired to make a move. And in that silence it began.

'Do you hear it?' Maddy murmured.

'Not with my ears,' Ralph replied.

'No . . . but . . .'

The sound intensified, throbbing through the air, wanting, longing to get out. Its pitch increased. Maddy began to rub her ears.

'It's the suitcase!' Her voice was a whisper now. 'The noise—it's coming from the suitcase!'

The three of them turned towards the suitcase which was in its old position beside the fireplace, where Uncle Alistair had placed it that afternoon. The twin snakes flickered on its lid. It seemed to draw their attention; they could not tear their eyes off it. They could only watch. Meanwhile the sound, high, bloodless, rang in their ears.

'I *had* hoped we'd finished for this evening,' said Uncle Alistair.

'How can we stop it?' asked Ralph.

Maddy stood up and approached the case.

'No, Maddy, you mustn't . . .'

But Uncle Alistair's warning came too late. Maddy opened the lid. A shadowy blackness spilled out from under the lid with a damp smell like rotting leaves. Maddy let out an astonished cry and put her hands to her face. The books shook in their shelves and papers rustled.

'No!' Uncle Alistair leapt forward. 'No! Get back! Get back at once!'

Suddenly, they all felt as if the room were slipping, beginning to tip, like the deck of an ocean liner about to sink beneath the waves.

'I have to close it!' shouted Uncle Alistair. 'I must! But get back! Get back!'

Noise rushed in Uncle Alistair's head like a torrent. He could scarcely hear himself speak because of the pounding in his skull.

The television screen shattered. The carriage clock on the mantelpiece jammed. Time stopped. That was when, as Uncle Alistair approached, like a helpless swimmer caught in a current impossible to resist, that was when . . . Out of the case, rising up, came arms. The arms were smooth and shone with the aura of a black star. The arms twisted forward, reaching, grasping, a whole octopus of them, more and more reaching out of the case.

Uncle Alistair stopped in his tracks. But by then there was no way back. He had no means of escape. The arms had him. They seized him, by his two elbows, by the shoulders, round the waist and across the mouth. Uncle Alistair struggled. Suddenly they had Maddy too. With a gargantuan effort, Uncle Alistair wrestled her free. He threw her onto the sofa beside Ralph, where she lay shaking. Ralph watched helplessly, unable to move.

The arms had Uncle Alistair firmly now, completely. His feet were lifted off the ground, though he was still struggling. Maddy and Ralph watched horrified as, despite his strength and efforts, Uncle Alistair was lifted horizontally and then steadily, gradually, pulled in through the open mouth of the case. Ralph closed his eyes. He could not bear to watch.

When he opened them, deep darkness welled in the bottom of the case once again. Glass from the TV had exploded in tiny pieces across the carpet. And where Uncle Alistair had stood only a moment before there was nothing. Uncle Alistair had vanished altogether.

9

After Uncle Alistair had gone Ralph and Maddy hardly spoke. They sat on the sofa, feeling sick and appalled, but what could they do? There was no one to ring—and no one to help them.

'So we do nothing?' asked Maddy.

She sat beside Ralph on the sofa with her arms curled round the cushions. Ralph was hunched under the blanket.

'Well,' he yawned, 'we can't do anything now.'

Ralph was annoyed, but tried not to show it. Losing his temper would only make both of them feel worse.

'You know...' said Maddy.

'What?'

'Uncle Alistair talked about something today—while you were at the Grange.'

'What was that?'

'He talked about sacrifice—when one thing is offered in place of another.'

'So?'

'Well, I *knew* I shouldn't open the case. I *knew*, but I did it, because I wanted to. It's hard to explain—but there, I've said it.'

'And?'

'Weren't you watching? Didn't you see? Those arms came for *me*. At least at first. But Uncle Alistair got in the way and pulled me out. So *he* went into the case instead of me. It was a kind of ... sacrifice. I think that's what he was talking about today. He didn't need to, he didn't have to, but he did it.'

'And where is he now?' asked Ralph.

'I don't know,' said Maddy. 'I only know he's where I should be. How on earth are we going to get him back?'

'Look, Maddy, maybe something will happen tomorrow and then we'll have a clue about what to do.'

'Maybe.'

'But I think we have to go to bed now, because there is absolutely *nothing* we can do. It's too late.'

Nothing. Nothing hung in the room like an accusing echo. There was Nothing in the case. There was Nothing they could do. Where Uncle Alistair had been—there was Nothing. Nothing. It all seemed hopeless to Maddy, and too heavy to bear.

'OK!' she agreed, reluctantly. 'We'll go to bed—but I don't think I'm going to get any sleep!'

Neither of them slept well. Maddy kept waking up. Ralph remembered looking at his clock at four. When he woke next morning he realized he must have dozed— but his eyes were heavy and he was weary and unrested.

At breakfast they felt lost without Uncle Alistair. Maddy put on the radio to fill the kitchen with sound.

'What should we do, then?' she asked helplessly. She could hardly bear to think about Uncle Alistair. She felt grumpy as well as tired. She poured out a bowl of cornflakes.

'Go into the village?' suggested Ralph, already onto his second bowl.

Maddy closed her eyes. No. She had spent the whole of the previous day in the village.

'I know!' said Ralph.

'What?'

'We can go and look at the painting in the schoolhouse.'

'Why? Didn't you get told off last time?'

'So? If there's nobody there we can have a quick look. I want to see if the knights have moved again.'

'Why?'

'Because—because the painting might tell us something. It might show us something we need to know.'

'You're beginning to sound like your uncle. The only moving pictures I like are videos. But I don't want to stay here, either. So we may as well go to the schoolhouse.'

Ralph went out of the house to wait for Maddy. The lawn was beginning to streak brown in the continual heat. Ralph yawned. There, in front of him, was a man. The man hovered in the drive. It was Mr Barnes. Ralph swallowed. Yesterday evening's conversation came back to him. Now he knew why this figure had been dredged up from his past. He realized what he should do—only it was difficult to speak.

'Mr Barnes,' said Ralph in a small voice. He coughed. The figure remained immobile. The man's eyes stared at Ralph, without recrimination or judgment. Ralph knew this *wasn't* really Mr Barnes, but a kind of picture from the past—yet he felt that Mr Barnes was waiting for something.

'Mr Barnes,' said Ralph again, 'it *was* me. I know you know it was me, and . . . it *was*! And I'm sorry.'

Ralph blinked and Mr Barnes had gone. It was as if someone had come and put an intense hand of light over Ralph's heart. The light burned into him, cold at first, and then warm. It was a warmth of forgiveness which spread right through him. Some kind of weight slipped off, a weight Ralph hardly knew was there and he felt better all of a sudden. He felt . . . free. The light set his heart beating and he wanted to jump and shout.

'Are you all right?' said Maddy, coming out and closing the door behind her.

'Never better,' said Ralph. 'Now, let's go to the schoolhouse!'

As they arrived, Ralph glanced across at the Grange. Maddy could see the distress on his face.

'At least Sir George doesn't like coming in here,' he said, lifting the latch on the gate.

They hurried up the stone path. A spangle of sunlight gleamed on the polished wood inside. There was nobody about.

'Look!' Maddy picked up a copy of the parish magazine lying on a chair. A notice on the back read: PLAYGROUP STOPS FIFTEENTH. STARTS AGAIN TWELFTH OF NEXT MONTH.

'Yesterday was the last day, then.'

'Good,' said Ralph firmly, 'no Mrs Williams.'

He swept aside the sheet that hung over the painting. All the plaster had been scraped off, but there was a good deal of close restoration work to be done.

'It *has* moved again!' Maddy took a step back.

'Yes!'

They both examined the painting. The knights appeared to have taken a gallop closer to the mound where the figure of Aelfric was lying. Their faces had turned outward, giving the illusion that all four of them were staring right at Maddy and Ralph. Inside the hollow, the black stars had massed round Aelfric into a black line. What was strangest of all— Aelfric had been lying on his back: now he was lying on his side.

'Why has he changed position?' asked Maddy.

'Maybe he's going to get up?'

'I thought he was supposed to stay asleep until the end of time.'

'Perhaps Sir George and his friends have disturbed Aelfric's sleep?'

Maddy shuddered.

'It's only a painting,' said Ralph.

But it was clear to them, clear beyond any doubt, that this was not *only* a painting.

'I think we'd better go now,' said Ralph. 'I don't want to get caught here twice.'

They were just leaving the schoolhouse when they bumped into Nick Fleming.

'Good morning to you! How's that uncle of yours?' he said.

'Fine,' lied Ralph.

'Good-oh! I could do with a word with him if you could get him to give me a ring.'

'Oh?'

'People in the village are getting excited. These—er—appearances have really stirred them up.'

'I'll get him to give you a ring then, but I think we're quite busy today.'

'Splendid! When he can!'

'What did you say that for?' Maddy hissed when Nick had disappeared inside. 'Uncle Alistair can't ring anybody!'

'What else could I say? Uncle Alistair's disappeared? Into a suitcase? Nick Fleming might be open-minded... but... you know...'

'Oh, I suppose you're right!'

They walked towards the gate. A breeze rippled the grass. An oldish man wearing a cap was standing in his shirt sleeves on the pavement. He was lighting a pipe and talking to a young woman who had a small child with her.

'... all of them,' he was saying, 'it was just one or two at first. Well, that wasn't so bad. But then my old dad turned up! It gave me quite a turn, I can tell you.'

'I know!' The woman shooed the child off to a distance. 'I hadn't seen ... well ... I didn't see ... until ... then there was one. A soldier. But now! The past couple of days an aunt of mine has appeared. There's this ...'

' ... like they want something,' finished the old man. 'I felt so small when my dad looked at me. We were never on the best of terms, and we parted that way when he died. I don't know, maybe seeing him again is a chance to get things straight and to get me straight. I'm going to say something if he comes again.'

The woman went very quiet. She paused. 'Maybe you're right,' she said in a chastened voice.

Ralph pulled Maddy along the pavement.

'We haven't been seeing anything much,' she said, 'not like them.'

'I have,' said Ralph.

'Oh?'

'I saw Mr Barnes this morning and I spoke to him.'

'And?'

'You have to speak to them and then they go away. But it ... changes you. I feel ... better, different.'

'There's ...' but Maddy did not need to finish. Ralph could tell she was staring across the road at the Grange.

'I don't want to hang about here,' said Ralph.

'Do you think Uncle Alistair's over there?'

'Who knows where Uncle Alistair is? He said that case was a tunnel, didn't he?'

Ralph tailed off.

'So how do we get him back?'

'I don't ... I don't ... know!'

They stopped walking and found themselves gazing over to the Grange once again.

'Why don't we go and have a look?' suggested Ralph.

'What?'

'At the Grange. There's a big garden. We could climb up and sit on top of the wall.'

'But you've already been inside.'

'Only one room and I couldn't see anything. Coming?'

Ralph began to saunter across the road.

'Ralph! Careful!' Maddy started to follow. 'Oh, all right! I'm coming!'

The Grange stood side on to the road, behind its wall. The front of the house faced a sweeping garden planted with large rhododendron bushes. On the far side of the Grange, by the wall which surrounded the house, was a right of way which led to Howsworth. A ditch ran alongside the path, bordered by nettles and cow parsley. Ralph and Maddy followed the footpath until they were some distance from the road.

'We should get up there easily enough,' Ralph said, nodding at the wall.

Maddy looked at the ditch—and the nettles. She hated being stung—but, raising her arms, she plunged into the thick of them.

Beech trees hung over the wall from the other side so that a curtain of leaves fell between them and the house. Ralph leapt across the ditch, scrambled up the loose bricks and gave a low whoop as he reached the top of the wall.

'Come and see!'

Maddy followed. Climbing had never been any problem for her. Ralph waited for her, crouched on the wall.

'It's wide enough to walk on,' he said.

'I can't see much.'

'So we go round.'

'Oh, Ralph!'

'Why not?'

'OK, but not too far round. Just enough to have a

decent view, all right?'

Stooping low, Maddy and Ralph edged along the top of the wall, behind the screen of beech trees. They proceeded slowly, avoiding the branches, so as not to shake the trees and arouse suspicion in the house.

'There!'

Ralph waved to Maddy to stop. Through the leaves they could see Sir George's house. The honey stone was warm above the lawn, and the white-painted window frames seemed fresh and inviting in the sun. On this side of the house was an extensive stone terrace with a flight of steps to the garden. The French windows leading out onto the terrace were open. People were coming in and out. A couple were seated on wicker chairs.

'How many people are there?' asked Maddy.

'I don't know. I saw about eight, but there are more.'

Ralph peered through the leaves. He recognized the woman with long black hair and the middle-aged man.

'They seem to be preparing for something,' said Maddy.

A few people were transporting strange objects into the house through the French windows.

'Come on!' Ralph beckoned. 'This is no good!'

In a flash he had clambered down the other side of the wall into the garden and dived into the bushes.

'Ralph!' hissed Maddy.

'Come down! Come on! They can't see us!'

'I—oh, all right—but if we get caught . . .'

'We won't get caught! Quick!'

Maddy scrambled down and joined Ralph. They advanced slowly towards the house. The huge banks of rhododendron afforded plenty of protection, only with the mass of twigs underfoot it was hard not to make a noise.

'I think this is as close as we get,' whispered Maddy.

'... if indeed it does work!' The words seemed to leap out of the undergrowth.

Ralph halted in his tracks. Maddy clutched his arm. He put his finger to his lips and froze. A few feet in front of them were two people sitting on the grass by the bushes. Maddy and Ralph could see their backs now. Maddy's face blanched.

'Why shouldn't it work?' It was the man talking. He sounded like one of those people who read the news.

'Because what we are trying to do...' the woman's voice was husky with a determined note in it.

The man broke in, 'What we are trying to do will change...everything. It will be the beginning of a new era!'

'Yes, but we don't have the final piece to complete the puzzle! That wretched man! Everything was under control till he turned tail and ran away!'

'But we can still manage.'

'So Sir George says.'

'Don't you believe him?'

'I believe in results!' The woman was impatient. 'I am long past the stage where I believe in people! If anything goes wrong...'

'What can go wrong?'

'I don't know whether to admire your confidence or to laugh at it!' she snorted. 'Sir George *thinks* he knows what he is doing. He thinks he will be able to take us to the end of time...'

'...and?'

'Sir George is excited by his own power. Excitement like that can blind a man.'

'Then why are you here?'

'I am here because I, too, want power. I know that what Sir George promises is real—but whether that reality will bend to us is another question. Our journey tonight will be a dangerous one, and there's been little talk of the danger—only of triumph. Why are you here?'

The man paused. 'I am here because ... there are some people ... I wish to take care of ...'

'I see. We should go back and help with the preparations. It won't do us any good to be missed.'

'No.'

Ralph and Maddy held their breath as the two rose. They watched them walk back across the lawn to the house.

'We go, right away!' Maddy insisted in a hot whisper in Ralph's ear.

'Don't worry,' said Ralph with a shiver, 'this is the last place I want to be now!'

'I don't like the sound of what they're planning.'

It was later. They were back in Uncle Alistair's house, sitting on the carpet by the sofa. Maddy was teasing out the ends of her hair.

'How are we ever going to get Uncle Alistair back?' Ralph said.

Maddy's face clouded as the pain of Uncle Alistair's absence flooded back.

'What do you think?'

'I don't know *what* to think!' Maddy was irritated again. 'Maybe ...'

'I think we just have to wait.'

While they waited, they tidied up the living-room and swept up the broken glass. The television with its punctured screen looked awful. The carriage clock would not start again. It was as though time had stood still.

The afternoon shadows lengthened. A thin veil of cloud began to pale the indigo sky.

'Why don't we just call Uncle Alistair?' Maddy said.

'What do you mean? This isn't one of your bright ideas, is it?'

'Listen—don't make fun of me. Why don't we try?'

'Try? Just like that? Just shout his name?'

'Well, *he* called *you*.'

'I know, but he does things . . . What did he do?'

'It was to do with the light. He took a lighted candle and shouted your name. Why don't we try that?'

'Maybe . . .' Ralph propelled himself across the floor to the suitcase.

'Ralph . . .' A warning edged into Maddy's voice.

'It'll be all right,' protested Ralph. 'It's not making a noise or anything.'

'I just think . . .'

'Why don't we try calling Uncle Alistair in the case?' asked Ralph, excitedly. 'The final piece of the puzzle.'

Maddy drew back, remembering the words of that woman in the garden.

'That's what those people at the Grange said,' said Ralph. 'And we have it. But what *is* the puzzle? I wish I knew what this thing is really for.'

Before Maddy could say anything, Ralph had lifted the lid of the case.

'Give me a candle, Maddy.'

Maddy lit a candle and handed it to Ralph. He stretched out his hand. Without a word, he leant over and put his head inside the case till only his neck showed above the rim.

'Uncle Alistair!' he called down into the echoless, black Nothing. He waved the candle. 'Uncle Alistair! We're here! The light. Follow the light!'

Ralph drew back his head. 'There, I've done it,' he said. Sweat stood out in drops on his forehead. 'And I'm not doing it again!'

'Close the case!' ordered Maddy. Ralph snapped it shut and blew out the candle.

'There,' said Ralph, 'that's that.'

He stood up. 'I'm going to the bathroom,' he said.

113

When Ralph came out of the bathroom, he heard a noise coming from the walls.

'It must be the pipes!' he told himself as he hurried back downstairs.

Maddy was standing with her back to the fireplace in the living-room. The thumping in the walls sounded again. Then again.

'Do you hear that?' said Ralph. 'What is it?'

'That's nothing,' said Maddy. 'Look!'

She was standing in front of the mirror above the fireplace. Instead of the usual reflection, the mirror had filled with a swirl of grey mist which was getting thicker. Soon it covered the inside of the glass.

'What's happening? Are all the mirrors like that?' asked Ralph. 'All over the house?'

'Let's check,' said Maddy, 'but don't get too close.'

She rushed into the hall, then the kitchen, and then had a look in Uncle Alistair's study while Ralph toured the rooms upstairs.

'Well?' he shouted down over the banister when he had finished.

'They're all the same down here. They've gone a sort of grey.'

'Same up here! What do you think is causing it?'

'How should I know?'

The insistent knocking in the walls sounded again. This time it was louder.

'I think . . . I . . .' Ralph gave a yell. 'Maddy! Maddy!' He bounded down the stairs. Maddy was standing in the hall. He dragged her into the living-room.

'What is it, Ralph?'

'It's . . .' Ralph pointed, 'well, it's that!'

Maddy's eye followed the line of Ralph's finger.

'Oh, no,' was all she could manage. Her face filled with dismay.

From the swirl of grey mist behind the mirror emerged the tips of human fingers. A hand groped blindly behind the glass and then another appeared out of the blankness. The two hands stretched out like a sleepwalker's. As Maddy and Ralph watched, trousers and a striped shirt became visible through the mist. Then the face—sightless, confused, disturbed—appeared. It was the face of Uncle Alistair.

'It's . . .'

'But where is he?' interrupted Maddy. 'Where can he be? He can't be behind the glass! He can't be in all the mirrors!'

But he was. Uncle Alistair was all over the house. He was in the kitchen, in the hall, and in every bedroom. From behind every mirror in the house, the face and form of Uncle Alistair stumbled out of the mist and began thumping on the other side of the glass. The knocking which they had heard before shook distantly in the walls. Uncle Alistair's lips moved in effort, but Ralph and Maddy heard no sound. Then, as they stood there, they heard the man's voice, thin and faint.

'Let me out! Let me out!'

'How can we let him out?' said Maddy turning to Ralph. 'How is that possible?'

'We could try smashing the glass.'

'If it would work. But not here. He'd have to climb over the fireplace.'

'I know! There's a full-length mirror on the wardrobe in Uncle Alistair's room.'

'Let's try that then.'

'Here!' Ralph and Maddy entered Uncle Alistair's bedroom, where he was still struggling to get out, pressing against the other side of the mirror.

'What can we smash it with?' Maddy demanded.

'A chair.'

'You try, then.'

Ralph lifted Uncle Alistair's bedside chair and hurled it against the mirror.

'Oh . . .'

'No, let me do it!' Maddy seized the chair from Ralph. 'I only hope this doesn't hurt him!'

With all the strength she had, Maddy hurled the chair against the glass. Spider-thin lines cracked across the mirror. But the glass did not break. Lifting the chair, Maddy tried once more. This time there was a dreadful splintering and the chair seemed to go through, into something, before falling back at Maddy's feet. Her heart was pumping frantically and she was breathing hard. She felt sick with the effort.

The mirror broke into pieces. Fragments of glass shattered and crashed to the carpet. Mist, cold and damp, the mist of ages, locked up in a deep cave for centuries, poured out. With it, a figure fell to the floor and lay unconscious.

Ralph coughed and stumbled to open the window. He could hardly see anything.

Maddy noticed that the glass of the wardrobe mirror backed only onto wood. The stench in the room was of old bones and battles and armour.

'Do you . . .' but Maddy stopped. She saw that Ralph was stock still. Then she saw too, in the clearing fog, what he was looking at. Bits of earth lay in scattered crumbs all over the bedroom carpet. A pair of leathery feet stuck out of the bottom of a ragged cloak, rotten and torn with age.

The person lying on the floor was certainly not Uncle Alistair. He had tousled hair and a streaked, matted beard. The man lay with mud-smeared arms stretched out in front of him. His clothes were ingrained with dust and in holes and tatters. As Ralph and Maddy stared, they knew there was only one person it could be. It was so obvious to both of them that neither really wanted to say it. In the end Ralph spoke.

'It has to be!—it has to be!' Ralph swallowed hard and looked at Maddy. 'It's the Black Warrior—it's Aelfric!'

10

Ralph stood with his back to the blowing curtains in Uncle Alistair's bedroom.

'So he *has* come back!'

Maddy plumped herself down to stare at the unconscious figure. Aelfric lay motionless at the foot of the wardrobe. His bulk seemed to fill the room. He was sprayed with earth and pieces of broken mirror.

'But he's still asleep.'

'For the moment, but who knows what's going to happen?' Ralph's voice was filled with foreboding.

Aelfric grunted. Maddy and Ralph jumped in shock. The man babbled something incomprehensible and rolled over onto his side.

'What if he does wake up? Won't he do terrible things?' Maddy took a deep breath.

'Probably.' Ralph was worried. 'But he might not wake up.'

Ralph bundled the duvet off Uncle Alistair's bed and spread it over Aelfric. The man shuffled his feet and snorted.

'I think he *is* waking up,' said Maddy.

'You may be right, but . . .' Ralph turned and held out his hands. 'We can't run away. We can't do anything. We can only stay and wait.'

A few minutes passed. Maddy glanced up at Ralph. 'Do you think it really was Uncle Alistair in the mirror—or was it just Aelfric trying to get out?'

'But Aelfric's asleep! How could he try and get out?'

Ralph shrugged.

Maddy sighed, 'Oh, this is too confusing!'

Ralph bent forward to examine Aelfric's face. The dark figure lay on the bedroom floor with the weight of a tree trunk. His limbs were sprawled like a drunken man. As he breathed, his chest rose and fell very faintly. Prickles rose on the back of Ralph's neck. Talking about Aelfric was one thing—learning about the painting in the schoolhouse and discussing his history—but to be face to face with a real person, that was quite another. Besides, Aelfric was supposed to be terrible—'without mercy', that was what Uncle Alistair had said. He had terrorized everyone in the Dark Ages and put people to the sword. What was worse, he was supposed to wake up 'at the end of time'. Ralph hardly dared imagine what that might mean.

Aelfric's face was sunken. His cheek-bones stood out above the hollows below. There were lines gathered under his eyes. His skin was parched and his whole body was powdered with fine, white dust. Aelfric's brow was powerful and strong. Ralph could imagine him as a warrior. But what had Aelfric actually done? Uncle Alistair had not gone into detail. And what had been happening to him all these long years asleep in the cave of black stars?

'I wonder *why* he came through the mirror,' said Ralph.

'*You* called.'

'That was *your* idea. Anyway, I shouted for Uncle Alistair. No, something must have happened to bring Aelfric closer. I couldn't have done it.'

'You mean Aelfric's appearance has to do with what's happening at the Grange?'

'I suppose so—it's tied up with Sir George and power ...'

' ... and the end of time—that's what the legend said. He'd wake up at the end of time ...'

Maddy came to a dead stop. For a moment she felt everything she had always taken for granted was under threat. It was as if the world were woven out of a single, seamless fabric and now that fabric was about to be torn. What lay on the other side of it? What lay outside her senses? What existed there? What *was* at the end of time?

Maddy had never thought about it before. How was it possible, anyway, to imagine beyond space and time to the very *end* of everything? Could there really be anything beyond that? Questions and fears which usually stayed distant came rushing close. Maddy knew that things had beginnings and ends. She knew that there was a start and finish to everything—but what about the start and finish of Everything? What was Sir George really after, and what would happen to them all if he got it?

'You've gone very quiet,' said Ralph at last.

'I know. I was thinking.'

Aelfric opened his mouth. He gave a loud yawn.

'He *is* waking up,' said Maddy.

Aelfric folded his hands under his head. His mouth sagged open, though his lips were hardly visible through his beard. He snored, and blinked half-consciously. He seemed to be trying to force himself awake. Behind his shrunken, pinched face some gargantuan effort was taking place.

'I don't like this!' said Maddy.

'Shh!' Ralph drew nearer the man and bent over him again.

Aelfric opened an eye. It was hazel, brilliant, and it pierced Ralph to the core. Aelfric stared at Ralph and the sheer force of his gaze knocked him back a few steps as though he had been punched in the chest.

'What is it?' asked Maddy in concern. She retreated to the door.

'Nothing,' said Ralph, 'just a minute.'

He crouched over Aelfric and watched as life returned to the warrior's face. A flush of colour spread across the man's white cheeks and his lips moistened. His breathing changed. More than that. As Ralph watched him, character seeped back into the man's features. Strength rounded his brow. Aelfric's face was gaunt, but impressive. It looked as if it had been hacked out of hundreds of battles and skirmishes. But there was something else, and it was this which caused Ralph to gape in wonder. Aelfric yawned and stretched out a dusty hand. His groping fingers parted. He opened his other eye—and his stare was like a gust of wind strong enough to lift you off your feet. There was power in Aelfric. He was extra-ordinary, that was clear, but . . .

'Oh!' said Maddy. She had come to stand beside Ralph. She sensed something too. When Maddy caught the expression on Aelfric's face, it struck through her to the marrow. She felt as if she would be knocked flying. It was so intense. The man's hazel eyes blinked. Maddy detected a smokiness in them—the smokiness of autumn when there is ripe fruit and the riches of the land are ready for harvest. A smokiness of damp, misty days when you want to go out and lose yourself in a wood, treading on the gold and yellow leaves at your feet. Days when everything seems good. But there was more than that. Still more.

In Aelfric's eyes they could see a steady flame, a flame which burned deep within him and brought life back to his sleeping body. Maddy recognized that flame. She had known it in the candles when they were beating back the shadows Sir George had sent. There was light in Aelfric! Light welling up inside him. It was *the same light which they recognized in Uncle Alistair*, the light he had talked to her about.

'Ralph . . . I . . .' stuttered Maddy.

'Yes,' said Ralph, quietly.

Aelfric wrestled himself into a sitting position. As he

yawned he showed blackened teeth. His great, shaggy head turned to Maddy and Ralph. He looked like a dishevelled lion, with its strength held in check. One swipe and Maddy and Ralph would have been done for. But there was care in the man's movements. His body throbbed with life. His lips fell open and he sighed. Maddy had never beheld such a face.

He had the face of a warrior, chiselled and rugged. An ugly scar ran down his left cheek and deep lines from old wounds were scored above his eyebrows. He looked fierce. But that was only on the surface. Beneath Aelfric's features, visible through them, was a kind of... suffering or pain. This marked him. Some great sadness dwelt in Aelfric—a sadness as deep as the sea. It washed over him and gave him a kind of faded beauty. His face spoke of power—and of great tenderness.

When Aelfric looked at Maddy and Ralph, it was as if he knew them from the *inside*. That made them squirm. It *is* uncomfortable to feel that someone can see into you and detect your faults and flaws. But Aelfric's gaze held no judgment. To have him look at you made you feel you were being drawn closer to the Light.

'He's not... he's not...' whispered Maddy.

'No,' said Ralph. His voice was stamped with bewilderment. 'He's not at all what we expected. He's not terrible—he's full of light. He's... changed...'

'But he *is* terrible,' contradicted Maddy.

'Yes,' nodded Ralph, 'because of the Light in him. It makes you feel you have to...'

'...change...' said Maddy. So Ralph recognized it too. She swallowed.

'Do you think he can speak?'

Aelfric screwed his eyes shut. He drew both hands over his face. He seemed weary. He turned to both of them.

'I speak!' The words tumbled from him in a pounding torrent.

'In the cave of black stars, my sleep was the sleep of . . . centuries. Can you comprehend that, little ones?'

Ralph shook his head. Maddy said nothing.

'No, it is a mystery too deep for the telling.' Aelfric groaned. 'In my sleep I was wrapped in a garment of dreams which followed the shifting patterns of the years above ground. So I beheld the passing of the centuries and my tongue was moulded to the changing fashions of speech. It was a gift for when I should awaken at the end of time.'

'Is . . . would you like anything?' asked Ralph.

'Water . . .' Aelfric's voice was hoarse and dry, like sandpaper.

'OK. One minute.'

Ralph dashed to the bathroom and filled a glass. Maddy was left alone with the warrior. She shrank from him. She was afraid.

'You are more silent than I,' he said.

Ralph came back and Aelfric cradled the glass in his massive hands. He gulped the water. It dribbled off the end of his chin.

'Can you walk?' asked Ralph. 'Maybe we should go down to the kitchen.'

'I can speak—I can walk!'

Aelfric offered Maddy and Ralph his thick arms and they tried to help him stand. He buckled, but then, shakily, managed to get to the landing and then down the stairs. He trod with careful dignity. He was as tall as a giant. Maddy found some bread and put it on a plate in front of him.

Aelfric kept his eyes on the window. The waving branches of the trees entranced him. The grass delighted him. He had not used his eyes for so long. Now he was dazzled by the glare of sunlight on the panes. He turned to Maddy and Ralph.

'A boy and a girl.'

'So?' said Ralph. He had heard that before—it was what the man with the suitcase had said on the train.

'Benedictus swore to me that a boy and a girl would be my only way out of the cave. Now I am with you.'

'I don't ... I don't understand,' said Ralph. 'I thought you were a warrior ...'

'I *am* a warrior!' Aelfric's eyes burned with a ferocity which took Ralph's breath away. His great shoulders heaved. There was something volcanic about him.

'Why have you come?' asked Maddy.

Aelfric seemed sad. 'Do you not know the tale of Aelfric? Does my name yet echo in these parts, or has it been laid to rest under the hills?'

'People do talk about you,' said Ralph, 'but they say you were a terrible warrior, terrible—without mercy.' Ralph shook. He did not know where he found the confidence to say this.

'And so I was!' said Aelfric. 'I slaughtered my uncle for his sword and with that sword I established my rule! All bowed the knee to Aelfric, all brought tribute to him. Those who stood against me I slew—aye—and others beside, to show the teeth of my wrath! No man could bring sword against me!'

'But what happened?' asked Ralph.

Aelfric shivered. Ralph helped him to a chair and the two sat down beside him.

'I climbed to gain a crown,' the old warrior continued, 'through killing, through blood, through treachery—and poison seeped into my own blood. My dreams grew troubled. Then I dared not sleep—for in sleep I feared the assassin's knife. Those I once trusted I viewed with suspicion. I smelled plots. The fruits of my power brought no joy. I was steeped in darkness.'

'And?' said Maddy.

'There came a man from over the sea. Benedictus was his name and his tongue was foreign. He was gentle, and the Light he brought smote the darkness of the gods we served and showed the truth at the heart of the world. Nothing could stand against this Light, he said; it was a light for every nation. He healed the sick; he called us to believe him. He was more to be feared than any sword! He challenged my power. "Come, fight!" I said to him, but he refused—his weapons were not of this world. I called him a coward. How I hated him! I had never met his like before! I felt the living Light in him—and knew that Light was calling me! It wanted me. I would have put it out if I could, because it demanded that I lay down my sword. But then ...'

'Then what?' said Maddy.

'Benedictus was a worker of wonders. I might not reject the Light, he said, until I knew it for what it was. I should have no peace until then, for peace was in that Light alone. The saint struck his staff against the hill on which we were standing. Three times he struck! He opened the cave of black stars, and I was blown inside. Such a mighty wind I could not resist! It uprooted the trees! It sent the horses flying! I struggled in fury against the light. So long I struggled! The pain of it! I longed to vanish into my own darkness.

'At last, I came to know what I truly was—for in the Light I could see myself—my misshapen soul. But the Light did not leave me, it stayed with me. One day I was calm. I saw where the Light was coming from and what the Light wanted. I must give myself up and be filled with the Light, I must leave behind the man I was and become something new. Thus, the darkness which had poisoned me was banished and my sleep became filled with peace.'
Aelfric bowed his head.

'But aren't you supposed to be asleep until the end of time?' asked Ralph. 'How is it that you've woken up?'

'Is this not the end of time?' said Aelfric. 'The hour is always approaching. How do you know it is not now?'

Maddy shuddered. Ralph merely bowed his head. The thought of the end of time weighed them both down.

'Some power came close to me where I lay. It disturbed me. At first I longed to wake. But I questioned the power and found it wanting. Once I would have recognized it as power like my own, but not now. They were dark hands which delved down into my sleep! Hands mighty enough to enter my cave! Then I knew this power was after me to enslave me! Why wake then? Better remain asleep than become servant to such as those! But then there came a greater disturbance, like a howling wind. I awoke—and I was here with you!'

'This power . . .' said Ralph.

'A greedy power that transforms men into monsters!' Aelfric said fiercely. 'There is a darkness all about this place.' He craned his head towards the window. 'I have sensed it in my sleep. I have been wary of it! These dark ones wish to loose what should not be loosed! They wish to part what should not be parted! They seek power and great glory for themselves—but their course is perilous!'

'So we really have to do something about what's going on at the Grange,' said Ralph to Maddy. He sounded dejected, tired.

'But *what?*' asked Maddy.

'Uncle Alistair would have known, but we still don't know where he is.'

'Who?' Aelfric's eyes narrowed in a question. 'What man are you speaking of?'

'My uncle,' explained Ralph. 'We thought you were him. At least, we thought he was trying to get to us, only it was you who fell out of the mirror.'

'Ah!' said Aelfric. A glimmer of understanding seemed to dawn in him. 'Surely this man is now asleep in the mound!'

'What?' Ralph shouted.

'He has taken my place in the cave of black stars! There is another asleep on the slab, for I am here with you. And his sleep will deepen the longer he lies there.'

'Then we have to get him out!' said Ralph, leaping to his feet.

Aelfric shook his head. 'There is no way from this world!'

'There was a way out,' said Ralph. 'There *must* be a way in.'

'You don't understand!' Maddy added. 'I was the one who opened the case! He's there because of *me*! We can't just leave him! Oh, Ralph, maybe *that's* what the case is for—a way to the cave of black stars! Sir George wanted to wake up Aelfric, didn't he?'

'Come through to the other room,' said Ralph to Aelfric. The giant lumbered to his feet as Ralph led the way.

Ralph showed Aelfric the case, then he opened it. Its black bottom swilled with Nothing. Aelfric shuddered. He seemed to recognize what lay within.

'I dare not enter again! The journey alone would kill me! Close it! Close it!'

Ralph snapped the case shut. The snakes gleamed like gold tongues of hungry fire.

'So?' said Ralph.

'This is a way,' said Aelfric. His face was the colour of chalk. He trembled and tugged at his beard. 'I did not think it possible. But I could smell the cave as I gazed into its depths.'

'How do we get there?' said Maddy.

Aelfric swung round and pointed to the large mirror hanging over the fireplace. 'Behold!'

The glass twisted. The surface of the mirror shimmered and clouded to pearl grey. When it cleared they could see into an ancient stone chamber lit with torches. In the middle of it stood a smooth slab which rose sheer from the flagstoned floor. A man lay asleep on the slab.

'Uncle Alistair!' said Ralph.

'It *is* him!' said Maddy.

'So that is the man! The way into the cave is not like any other. It is dangerous to attempt it. But you tell me this man offered himself in your place. That is a precious thing. There is a power in such a sacrifice—a life laid down for others—which can defeat all the dark armies of the world. For it is something they do not understand. That power will aid you in your journey.'

Aelfric took a deep breath. 'Open that thing!'

Ralph bent down and opened the case. Aelfric was solemn, subdued, obviously uneasy at the black emptiness of the case. He looked at Maddy and Ralph with burning intensity.

'You must go in! There is no other way! To reclaim this man, you two must summon your courage to enter the cave of black stars!'

11

The black rectangle of the open case at Aelfric's feet drew their attention like a magnet. Sweat stood out on the warrior's brow as he tried to avoid seeing into its depths. He was disturbed at coming close to his prison-chamber again.

'We have to go in there?' Maddy gulped.

Ralph gazed in. Somewhere in the depths of blackness he detected the distant flicker of shifting constellations and the smell of the cave Aelfric had talked about.

'We can't just throw ourselves in!' he said.

'No,' said Aelfric, 'the way is hidden. Yet I have the power to uncover it. Look again, little one! You must learn to use eyes that see!'

Ralph blinked. In what should have been the bottom of the case were steps leading down into the gloom.

'Oh!' said Maddy.

'How are we going to see down there? We need a torch!' said Ralph.

'Couldn't we tie a string here and unroll it as we go in?' suggested Maddy.

'We don't have any string,' snapped Ralph.

'Little ones,' interrupted Aelfric, silencing them, 'you cannot enter the cave as you would any other place. Can you not understand? The chamber is not *in* this world.'

Ralph struggled to understand. Surely the steps went *somewhere*? The dizzying gap at his feet made him uncomfortable. Waves of sickness passed through him. He had a terrible fear that the darkness might rise to swallow him.

'How do we get there, then?'

'If you trust in yourselves, you will fail. And fire and flame are useless to you. To find a way through the darkness you must follow another light.'

'And Uncle Alistair's in there?' said Ralph.

'I hear him breathing even from here. With each beat of his heart he retreats further and further into the country of dreams.'

'Can we wake him?' asked Maddy.

'You must try,' said Aelfric.

'What do we do?'

'You must command him to awaken. That is all. If you get as far as the cave, you will be obeyed.'

'We have to go in then,' said Ralph.

He was about to plunge in when something happened in the mirror above the fireplace. Uncle Alistair, the slab and the torches shimmered and vanished under threads of mist.

'What's happening?' asked Maddy.

'I do not know,' said Aelfric.

'It can't be doing that by itself!' said Ralph.

The mist darkened and cleared to reveal a familiar garden of rhododendrons and beech trees. The last of the evening sun lit the lawn.

'The Grange!' whispered Maddy.

As they looked, they could see figures walking through the rooms, intent on the purpose which had brought them so far. The preparations were almost complete. Something was beginning.

'What place is that?' gasped Aelfric.

'The Grange...' said Maddy.

'It is... the dark hands in the cave—they came from there. It is a place of great danger!'

'I know!' said Ralph.

'We must not be drawn to look further! No good will come of it!'

Aelfric lifted a hand and the image of the Grange blurred and vanished. A mist swept across the glass. The mirror reflected Uncle Alistair's living-room once more.

'The gift of sight is a precious thing. But to be given the gift of seeing into dark and hidden places—that brings with it a terrible responsibility. That place is the source of the disturbance I felt as I lay entombed!'

'We must go!' said Ralph. The thought of Uncle Alistair sinking further and further into sleep spurred him on. He didn't want to waste any time.

'Well, if we're going, let's go!' said Maddy. 'After me!'

With that, she brushed Ralph aside and walked down the worn stone steps into the darkness. The blackness swallowed her to the shins, to the waist, to the shoulders... Then she had disappeared completely into the case.

'There are tunnels which run from the entrance,' said Aelfric. 'The cave is not gained easily. But remember this—follow the left hand at every turn!'

Without a single backward glance Ralph plunged in after Maddy.

'But beware the cave!' Aelfric's voice came echoing after them. 'Your uncle sleeps and the cave will be full of dreams!'

Once they were at the bottom of the steps the entrance seemed to hover behind them like a high window of light. Where they were standing there was an all-pervading smell of earth and dampness. They heard drips plopping ahead of them. The ground beneath their feet was uneven, the dips and hollows filled with stagnant water.

'I can't see a thing!' Maddy's voice boomed down the

long tunnel. 'Where do we go?'

'Aelfric said keep to the left.'

'That's a big help. I still can't see a thing!'

'It's our only hope. Where are you, anyway?'

'Here!'

Maddy stretched out her hand until she found Ralph.

'There . . .' he stepped nearer to her. Even though he could not see her, Ralph could hear her breathing. 'Let's see how far we get.'

They began to move forward in the blinding blackness. Behind them the window of light receded till they were in total darkness.

'Wait!' said Maddy suddenly.

'What is it?'

'A wall!' Maddy's free hand pressed against solid rock.

'So go left. Is there anything on your left?'

'I don't think so.' Maddy let go of Ralph's hand and groped outwards with both hands. She found nothing.

'Right, let's go that way, then.'

'If you say so.'

The ground was fairly smooth now and started to run downhill in a gentle slope. No boulders or large stones blocked their path. Feeling their way along the tunnel wall, they pushed their hands against the rock and inched forward in the pitch darkness. Maddy was terrified she would bump into something, or fall into something— or—even worse—that something would rise up and bump into her. It was only the thought of Uncle Alistair that kept her going. Uncle Alistair imprisoned in the cave—and all because of her!

Maddy stumbled and Ralph caught her. 'We're almost there,' she said.

Ralph had felt his senses sharpen in the darkness. He had become acutely aware of every sound, every drip. Then he saw, too. A few feet ahead of them, a light, greenish and phosphorescent, glowed from the walls. As they approached it, they began to see the dim outline of the tunnel.

'They're rocks,' said Maddy. 'Those lights! Look!' She brushed her fingers against the glowing stones.

The stones were dry and sharp to the touch. Each one seemed to bristle with a thousand edges. Ralph looked more closely at them. The stones were tiny, hardly the size of small marbles. Many were smaller still. Here in the tunnel they gave off an ethereal glow which gave both Maddy and Ralph a kind of livid green colour.

'Yuk!' said Maddy.

The light clung to them as they moved. It was almost as if the same greenish light began to shine out of their own clothes. Ralph tried to brush the glow from his sleeves, but that was useless. It had stuck fast.

'Do you think it's dust or what?' he asked.

'Who cares?' said Maddy. 'At least we can see now.' She tugged at her hair. Even that had begun to glow faintly.

They carried on. A smaller tunnel disappeared to the right into deeper darkness but they ignored it. Keep to the left! Keep to the left! Aelfric's words were their only guide.

Eventually they turned another bend, so sharp it seemed the tunnel was doubling back on itself. The light was faint here, but enough to see a few steps ahead.

That was when Maddy screamed.

'What is it? What is it, Maddy?'

Ralph saw her struggling, trying to break free from something just ahead of him. She had been walking with her eyes fixed on the gaping darkness when, without warning, a hand had thrust its way out of the wall and grabbed her by the wrist.

'It's—it's—oh, no!' She pulled harder.

Ralph rushed forward to help her. He found himself held fast by two hands which had risen out of the floor.

They clung to him below the knees. He began to kick and push, but they only gripped him tighter.

'Wait!' shouted Ralph. 'Don't struggle! Stand still!'

'But . . .'

'Just try it!'

'OK, if you say so.'

Maddy relaxed her hand. When she looked again, there was only a wall. The hand had gone. Ralph walked forward to where she was standing.

'How did that happen?'

'I don't know,' said Ralph. 'But if Benedictus put Aelfric in here, it can't be that bad a place. Besides, this place is full of dreams, isn't it? Maybe nothing is real. Maybe we're just seeing it in a special way.'

'Come on! If I stand here too long I won't want to go any further!'

Maddy set off again ahead of Ralph, keeping to the side of the tunnel. The glowing stones grew larger the further they walked.

'How are you doing?' asked Ralph.

'Recovering,' said Maddy. 'I got a shock. How long do you think we've been here?'

'I don't know—but maybe there isn't any time here. Maybe it's different.'

'You mean we could get back to the house at a completely different time . . .'

' . . . or in no time at all. Uncle Alistair said Sir William Fenton believed that Aelfric's Hollow was "out of time", whatever that means.'

'So we're in a place that doesn't exist.'

'We're in a place that *shouldn't* exist—but it does. It must exist in another way.'

'What way?'

'How should I know?'

'I don't know either. Oh, look!'

Maddy put her hand on the rough surface of one of the stones. Ralph stood behind her to see what she was looking at.

'There are other colours in them now!'

Rainbow colours sparked and shifted in the stones. There was a fire in them and the flames took on different shapes the longer you looked at them. Maddy saw trees and a field. Ralph saw a town street. The fire fanned and formed itself into figures. Maddy recognized the field, high and golden, and a romping brown dog.

'Ralph, they're ... memories ... in the stones. If you look at them long enough they ...'

But Ralph had already realized. He remembered the cobbled street from long ago.

'No,' said Maddy, 'I don't want to look any more!'

Look any more, more ... Her voice slid down the walls of the tunnel over the stones.

'There's a funny echo here!' said Ralph. *Echo here, here.*

'What do you ...?'

Do you, do you, you ... But then Ralph and Maddy saw a figure rising up in front of them. A sword flashed. Ralph took a step back.

'That looks too real for me,' he said.

'Ralph, it can't be any worse than ...'

The figure began to run towards them down the tunnel, his sword held in front of him. They could not see his face.

Trust, Aelfric had said. Follow the Light. But Maddy was at a loss. 'There must be something we can do!' she thought, but her mind had jammed.

And then she had it. Into her mind rose the one thing, the obvious thing, she could do. Without a word to Ralph she picked up one of the glowing stones from the tunnel floor and held it up. It pulsed in her hand like a star.

'The light beat back the shadows,' she said to herself.

'What can it do here?'

There was a blinding flash. The stone seemed to explode, cold, in her palm. Ralph turned away. Maddy was suddenly bathed in an intense light. It swirled up and down the tunnel. The figure halted in his tracks. He sheathed his sword and was gone.

'How did that happen?' said Ralph.

'A mixture of Uncle Alistair and Aelfric,' said Maddy. She laughed.

'What's so funny?'

'Nothing. I sort of knew what to do all of a sudden, but I didn't think it would work, that's all. We'd better get a move on.'

Ahead of them the tunnel widened out. Finally, in the rock, there was an entrance cut square and covered with a curtain.

Ralph thought of something he'd done at school, about ancient burial mounds—a long tunnel, and then . . .

Maddy shrugged at Ralph. 'I suppose we have to go in.' She lifted the heavy curtain, which was thick and patterned like a rug. They both had to bend down to enter.

Inside was a high, round room. A circle of burning candles hanging from the ceiling gave off a flickering light. Hangings—gold and turquoise and crimson—of woven cloth decorated the walls.

Ralph moved forward. He felt a soft, warm breath against his arm.

'What on earth?'

In the dim light he saw a horse's head beside him. The horse lay snorting under an embroidered rug. A medieval knight in full armour lay stretched on a fur beside the animal. The armour glittered in the shifting candlelight, but the knight did not move at all.

'Do you think . . .' said Ralph.

'He's one of the knights from the painting,' said Maddy. 'Look, there are four of them!' As their eyes got used to the light they saw the other horsemen through the gloom.

Ralph went over to the nearest knight. His visor was down and his metal gauntlets were folded over his breastplate. He could have been a statue beaten out of iron.

Maddy gazed up at the domed ceiling of the cave. Shadows flowed in ceaseless motion over the stone from the candles. They swirled and mingled like currents in a river—as if they had a life of their own.

Ralph stopped. There, in the centre of the cave, was a stone slab, and on that slab a man lay curled up, asleep.

'Uncle Alistair!' he breathed.

'I'm not sure . . .' Maddy began, but Ralph had already taken a few steps across the flagstones towards the stone slab. A snake hissed at him. Bats flew about him. He backed and turned round. Suddenly he was far away from Maddy. He blinked. In an instant, he was standing next to her again.

'Careful, Ralph,' she said, 'one step at a time!'

She and Ralph took one step forward. Nothing happened. Then another.

'That's it—there are different rules here,' said Maddy. She pushed Ralph ahead of her. They walked forward, but as they did so the slab seemed to get further away. It was as if it had fallen down the wrong end of a telescope. Then it loomed up again and they were pushing, pushing, against some kind of invisible wall. They were pushing, pushing at air, pushing at nothing at all. Yet it took all of their effort and sucked all their strength.

'There!' Maddy fell forward and stumbled to the ground. The wall had broken or given way. Great, deep gasps tore out of her. Ralph also felt the wall give way as he fell to his knees.

'We—are—here!' Maddy could scarcely speak.

The slab rose beside them. Ralph pulled himself up. The sleeping man now lay only a hand's length from him.

'Uncle Alistair!'

Uncle Alistair lay on the slab as though dead. He was hardly breathing. His eyes were sealed shut and there was no movement. His face had such a pallor that, if he had been examined in a hospital, the doctor would have shaken his head and said there was no hope.

Maddy put her lips to his cold, bloodless ear. 'Uncle Alistair!' she hissed.

Ralph shook his uncle, but the body was loose and lifeless. Wondering what to do, Ralph stared up at the high, domed ceiling. In the glitter above the candles, as though rising from the shadows, he saw crumbling and forming figures, colours, a pageant of memories and past places. Aelfric's words came back to him: 'Beware the cave . . . dreams.' But these were Uncle Alistair's dreams—wonderful, glorious dreams that soared higher than a vast cathedral roof. To the end of time they rose, and far beyond. At that moment Ralph had an inkling, just an inkling of what was terrible and wonderful beyond the end of time. He felt strong and alive, filled with light. Ralph looked down at his uncle. In a commanding voice he said: 'Awake!'

Uncle Alistair was floating far in space. He rolled in the infinite black where the arms that reached from the case had taken him. The arms had shrivelled but he had been abandoned . . . He had tried, but had been thrown back—back beyond planets and suns into the deepest black beyond the galaxy. The black was without stars until Uncle Alistair realized—no—the black *was* a star! So he had swum, swum without consciousness—then—from far away—he heard a voice calling him.

'Uncle Alistair!'

Before the black engulfed him completely, within and without, he knew he must push himself in the direction of that voice. Where that voice came from, there was light . . . he must reach for the Light.

And a voice said, 'Awake!'

Uncle Alistair's body trembled. He lay still for a moment. Then he coughed, moaned and shook his head. He awoke.

'Maddy! Ralph!' he mumbled. 'How—where? Those arms from the suitcase! The fall!'

'We're *here*—with you,' said Ralph quietly, 'not at your house.'

'Where is "here"?' Uncle Alistair sat up and rubbed his eyes. He winced and passed a hand across his brow as though he had a dreadful headache. 'Oh, I feel as if I've really been knocked out.'

'You have!'

'Where did you say we were?'

'In the cave of black stars—' said Maddy.

'—where Aelfric was,' added Ralph.

'Aelfric—Aelfric, the Black Warrior?' Uncle Alistair was confused. 'Then . . . where . . .?'

'Aelfric is waiting for us.'

'What!'

'There's a lot to explain.'

'He isn't terrible any more,' said Maddy. 'Somehow he woke up and you came here.'

'How very curious!' was all Uncle Alistair could manage.

'Do you think you can get up?' Ralph offered his uncle a hand.

'Yes, yes, I dare say. How do we get out of here?'

'Careful!' said Maddy, helping him off the slab.

Uncle Alistair walked between Maddy and Ralph,

hanging on to them. He stumbled along and had to stop for breath every few steps. It took a long time to get from the slab to the entrance of the cave.

Just as Maddy was about to duck her head to get out, a horse's whinny broke the silence. The animal's chestnut flanks trembled.

'They're waking up!' said Ralph. 'We must have disturbed them.' One of the knights unfolded his metal arms. His sword with its jewelled hilt lay at his feet.

Uncle Alistair turned round.

'Don't go back!' warned Maddy.

'It's all right!' Uncle Alistair extended a hand. In a moment the horse lay still again and the knight stopped moving.

'What did you do?' asked Maddy.

'I showed them we were friends.'

'Now,' said Ralph, 'let's hope we can find the way back.'

Ralph and Maddy and Uncle Alistair walked back up the long, glowing tunnel. 'If you see any . . .' But Ralph was cut short. Over their heads and around them they heard a screeching high-pitched screaming.

'What on earth . . .' exclaimed Maddy.

'Ignore it,' said Ralph, 'here, we . . . oh . . .'

Figures appeared ahead of them—a band of warriors wielding sticks and swords and knives. The group yelled and rushed towards them.

'I . . . I . . .' Maddy stuttered.

But Uncle Alistair held out a hand and they vanished.

'Down here,' said Ralph, 'but it gets dark now.'

The three of them quivered as they plunged back into utter darkness, feeling along the wall again. At last, after what seemed an age, they saw the tiny swimming window of light ahead of them. Fresh air washed their faces.

'There's a flight of steps,' said Ralph.

Ralph and Maddy made Uncle Alistair go first. He stumbled up and Maddy climbed after, followed by Ralph.

They lay on the living-room carpet drinking in the air, shielding their eyes from the electric light. The blackness of the open case swam beside Ralph.

'Close it! Close it!' he groaned. Maddy reached over and pushed the case shut.

The room felt solid and secure. Ralph bunched his hands into fists and waited for his stomach to settle. Outside the stars hung suspended in the sky and the countryside was sleeping.

'You succeeded!' said Aelfric.

'How long did we take?' asked Maddy.

'No time at all,' said Aelfric. 'The cave is subject to another set of laws.'

'I see,' said Maddy, though she did not see at all. As she lay on the carpet she gazed through the window at the endless sky. Soon, she told herself, she would be able to stand up.

'Night is falling,' said Aelfric. 'We must journey to that house. There is little time.'

'What house?' queried Uncle Alistair.

'The Grange,' said Ralph.

'The house that was shown in the glass,' Aelfric said.

'Why?' asked Maddy.

'Because, little one,' Aelfric's face stiffened, 'because I know. I can tell. The hours left to us are short. Something very horrible is beginning!'

12

Aelfric looked out of place in Uncle Alistair's living-room. He stood in front of the mirror, his eyes serious, his expression urgent. His words hung in the air: *'Something very horrible is beginning'*. He turned towards Uncle Alistair; Maddy and Ralph waited.

'You are the man, Alistair?'

'I am!'

Aelfric greeted him. 'It is no small thing these two have accomplished in bringing you back from the cave of black stars!'

'Indeed.' Uncle Alistair smiled and stood up. Aelfric was a good head taller even than he was. 'I can't tell you how good it is to return. I had no idea *what* had happened. The minute I was pulled into the case everything went black.'

The wind had risen outside and they could hear it whistling under the eaves of the house.

'The weather's changing,' said Maddy.

'Let's hope it gets rid of this heat,' said Ralph.

'Something's changing, anyway,' said Uncle Alistair.

He and Aelfric faced one another. Uncle Alistair was tall, his limbs slim and quick. He was wiry and concentrated to his fingertips. Aelfric, in contrast, was a full, powerful figure with broad shoulders. Even in such tattered garments he possessed a striking nobility. His head was fine, though his beard was wild, and his arms were muscular.

Just by looking, you could feel the strength in Aelfric. With Uncle Alistair it was different. Power was hidden behind an everyday appearance, ready to burst out. Uncle Alistair kept unexpected things in reserve.

The two men stared at each other, but said nothing. A deep stillness hung over both of them. Outside, the wind blew up a shoal of clouds to blur the moon and muffle the sky.

Uncle Alistair spoke. 'I see,' he said, 'you are not what you were. You have changed. Darkness to light. You have confounded us all!'

'What do you mean?' Maddy asked, puzzled.

The gleam of a smile played about Uncle Alistair's lips. 'Sir George and his friends—like all of us—were expecting Aelfric to awaken as a bloodthirsty warrior. Sir George thinks that Aelfric will be on his side, and help him in his quest to gain power at the end of time. But Aelfric, as you see, is no longer what he was. He is no longer on Sir George's side! The Light has changed him!'

'The Light that burns in me now,' said Aelfric, 'no darkness can put out! That Light comes from beyond the end of time where the hands of darkness can never reach!'

'Exactly!' said Uncle Alistair. 'The Black Warrior has become a warrior of light!'

'We must all become warriors of light!' said Aelfric. 'Is that not the task which lies before us? Is that not the way we should seek?'

It came to Maddy in that moment that Uncle Alistair too, in his own way, was a warrior of light. Looking at him now, with Aelfric, Maddy sensed it was the Light which bound them together.

'We ought to go now,' she said.

She stared through the bay window across the river and the darkened fields. The carriage clock on the mantelpiece was still jammed and she had no idea what time it was, only that the minutes were ticking by. The wind whistled round the chimneys.

'The Grange.' Uncle Alistair hesitated.

'What are we going to do when we get there?' demanded Ralph. 'What *can* we do?'

'I have no idea.'

'We have to do *something*!' Maddy sounded determined.

'But we don't need to know *what* till we get there,' said Uncle Alistair, gently but firmly.

It was typical of Uncle Alistair to wait and trust, Maddy thought, when she wanted to forge ahead and *act*. She thought of the darkness gathering outside the house. Her mind turned to the Grange and what was beginning there—the horrible thing—the thing which Sir George and those assembled with him had come to do. It frightened her.

The darkness Sir George was about to embrace was a darkness far deeper than the darkness outside Uncle Alistair's house. It was a darkness which would suck in the stars and the moon and leave no light to see by. It was a darkness which would turn the world cold. The very fabric of time would be torn and an old, raging power would come rushing in like a torrent. The thought chilled her.

'The Grange . . .' said Ralph.

'There is a shield of darkness surrounding that place,' said Aelfric. 'They want no one to see what is taking place. I swear they will part the curtain of time to steal what power they can find. But it is a dangerous game, for whatever they unharness they may not be able to control.'

'What do you mean?' Maddy asked.

Uncle Alistair explained. 'What Aelfric means is that Sir George might let loose something dangerous, something very destructive. These could be our last moments of ordinary time.' Uncle Alistair was grave. 'No one really knows what will happen if the curtain of time is parted. Sir George thinks it will be like finding a treasure trove and picking what he fancies. He thinks that time limits us and keeps us in our place, here in the world. Once he is free of time, he believes he will be able to obtain enormous powers—that *other* people will have to do what *he* wants.'

'But what else could happen?' said Ralph.

'If you make a hole in time,' said Uncle Alistair, 'it could be that everything that's here could rush out there—or perhaps the power that's out there could rush in here, unchecked. It could destroy everything! How can we tell?'

'But doesn't Sir George *know* that?' asked Maddy.

'Many are willing to risk all to attain absolute power,' said Aelfric.

'I think we should be making tracks,' said Uncle Alistair firmly.

'Right!' Ralph was ready, if uncertain. Maddy waited beside him.

The wind outside rose higher and battered the house. It screeched over the tiles. The window frames rattled and the trees in the drive swayed and rustled.

'It's wild out there!' said Maddy.

'What about the . . .' Ralph was about to say 'case' when he swallowed and stuttered to a halt. The gold snakes on the suitcase lid glistened. The warm light played on their fascinating forms. Ralph saw their tongues begin to lick. He looked on, horrified.

'The snakes!' he cried.

The creatures slithered round each other. One of the snakes lifted its head from the case. It wound out in a curve from the lid.

'Be careful!' warned Uncle Alistair.

The snake's eyes glowed with a sinister, emerald light.

Ralph thought he recognized those eyes. They reminded him of Sir George.

'Turn your heads away at once!' yelled Uncle Alistair. 'Don't look at that snake's eyes whatever you do! It will try and entice you towards the case. Don't move!'

Ralph faced the wall and placed his hands over his eyes. Behind him he heard the dry uncoiling slither of the snake and its slow, laboured hissing. From the top of the case rose a smell like musk, heavy and overpowering, which made Ralph's eyes water and swim.

'No!' said Uncle Alistair. 'We must ... we must ...', but Ralph could hear his uncle's voice choking. Consciousness was beginning to slip away from him under great, grey waves of sleep.

'I'm going,' he thought, 'I'm going ...'

'This must not be!' Aelfric's voice thundered out. He turned and strode towards the case. The snake's green eyes glinted at him. Aelfric trembled, halted in mid-pace by the creature's mesmerizing glow, but he drove himself on. His feet grew heavier as he advanced and the room darkened around him. All he could see clearly were the two points of the snake's eyes, calling him, calling him ...

'You have ... no place here!' Aelfric roared. He seized the snake by the neck. All at once a pure light glowed from his fist, the same light which had exploded from Maddy's stone in the tunnel. The snake extended its jaws to strike, but the light burned it up. It tried to coil round Aelfric, but the burning light blackened its tail to a crisp until, finally, it fell as ash from Aelfric's grip. The other snake ceased moving: it was just a design on the suitcase lid.

Ralph made sure that the second snake was definitely *not* moving before he dared approach the case. 'Should we take this with us?'

'It's dangerous ...' said Uncle Alistair.

'We must take it!' urged Aelfric. 'It is what we have.'

'And it was ... given to us, or at least left with us,' added Maddy.

'You're right,' said Uncle Alistair. 'We'd better get going! We'll take the footpath through the fields to the far side of the Grange. Follow me!'

Uncle Alistair led the way as they crossed the lane at the end of the drive and took the path across the fields. Maddy had a torch which cast a dim light on the few feet ahead of them. High above, the winking lights of a plane crossed the horizon. When they reached the footpath to the village, Uncle Alistair and Aelfric hung back a little, speaking in low voices that neither Maddy nor Ralph could hear. They went on talking until at last Ralph halted to let his uncle catch up.

'What do you think we're going to find?' he asked.

'I really don't know.' Uncle Alistair was thoughtful. 'If they've thrown a shield round the Grange it might be hard to get in. And we don't really know how much Sir George knows, but he has already summoned up a great deal of power. Still, he hasn't got everything his own way. The suitcase—which was to have provided the means of entering the cave of black stars—was never delivered. Without it Sir George made mistakes. And Aelfric is here with us, not with Sir George.

'The people at the Grange are in a hurry, and they're greedy, too—that may cause them to make more mistakes. The fact that Sir George is working blind gives us a chance to stop them. It's a small chance, I grant you, but it's still a chance!'

They crossed a stile and were now on the path which ran alongside the Grange. The wind dropped and, as they got nearer the Grange, the air thickened round them. It pressed like jabbing fingers till it hurt. It took more and more effort to go on walking. A stitch twinged in Maddy's side.

147

'It's the shield,' said Uncle Alistair. 'We ought to take care!'

'We'll be at the Grange in a minute,' said Ralph.

At last the wall to the Grange loomed from the mottled shadows on their right. They looked up the path towards the High Street. The road ahead was deserted. The schoolhouse was quiet. In the distance they saw a man walking his dog. He disappeared down the High Street.

They stopped, exhausted and gasping for breath. The pressure squeezed their lungs. It was dark by the Grange. They moved back until they were out of sight of the road. Uncle Alistair stood under the wall and listened.

He raised his hand. 'Can you hear? They have begun!'

He shut his eyes in pain. Such a weight of darkness there was in that place! Such a weight pressing down! Aelfric became very still.

Ralph sensed a faint rhythm coming over the wall, through the trees. The beat was strong, but the words weren't clear. He could pick up only pieces—syllables of words. It was impossible to fit the whole together.

'We should climb the wall,' Ralph said.

'What?' Uncle Alistair raised his eyebrows.

'There's a place over there.' Maddy pointed. 'It's easy to get on to the wall. They can't see us from the house but we can see what they're doing.'

Uncle Alistair hesitated. He did not ask how they knew. 'All right,' he agreed, 'let's try that.'

Ralph hoisted himself up and Maddy scrambled after him. Somehow, off the path, the pressure was less. They had pushed through to the other side of the shield. They both crouched on the wall and looked in the direction of the house. Nothing stirred. They turned and waved to Uncle Alistair to follow them.

Uncle Alistair handed up the suitcase. With a few agile movements he was seated on the wall with his legs dangling down into the dark of Sir George's garden.

'It's easier up here, isn't it?' he said.

'Yes,' said Ralph, 'I can breathe.'

'What about Aelfric?' Maddy whispered in concern. 'I think he may need some help.'

Aelfric was strong, but not supple. The stiffness of centuries of sleep clung to him. It took all three of them to help pull him up.

'Come on, Aelfric,' urged Maddy. 'Reach higher! There! That's fine!'

'Try to dig in with your feet...' encouraged Uncle Alistair. The warrior was enormously heavy.

Aelfric clung to the crumbling side of the wall. With an enormous effort, he hauled his great bulk to the top.

'There's the house,' said Ralph, pointing.

Uncle Alistair peered through the waving branches towards the house. All the windows were standing open and there was a glow of light. Above the stone balcony, the room behind the French windows was crammed with people. Ralph and Maddy could see their backs, about twenty or thirty in all. Sounds drifted from the house, but in fits and starts. The guests inside shifted and murmured. They raised their arms. They seemed to be chanting something.

'We'll have to get closer if we want to hear properly,' said Uncle Alistair.

'We can creep through the bushes,' suggested Ralph. 'That way they won't see us. Anyway, they won't think...'

'...no, they won't. Not at this hour. Well, let's try...'

'But what if...' Maddy bit her tongue. She did not finish what she wanted to say. She was frightened, but she knew as well as any of them that there was no time now for 'what if'.

Uncle Alistair climbed down first. Ralph and Maddy helped Aelfric, then they slid down into the flower bed beside the two men. They moved into the enveloping banks of rhododendrons under cover of the darkness, and started to walk towards the Grange, twigs crackling under their feet.

At last they reached the very edge of the thick banks of bushes. Pausing only a moment, they slipped onto the lawn one by one. Scurrying low past the windows to a large beech tree which dominated the lawn, they hid in its shadow.

They were much nearer the Grange now than Maddy and Ralph had been before. They could see clearly what was happening in the house.

Candles brimmed in every room. Black candles with black flames whose strange light danced in the shadows on the lawn. From where they were standing, the four could see that the guests inside had formed some kind of circle. They seemed to have assembled from many different countries. They were chanting in hypnotic rhythm. Faces blank of all expression, they appeared to be in a trance. The frenzy increased. They were shouting something over and over again.

'The end of time!'

'The end of time!'

They lifted their hands in triumph and cried out.

'What is it?' asked Ralph. 'What are they saying now?'

Aelfric put a trembling hand to his head. The chanting seemed to sap his strength. He appeared giddy and leant against the tree trunk. He let out a long moan.

Uncle Alistair turned to Aelfric. 'It's you they want, isn't it?' he said.

Aelfric's voice dried in his throat. He could only nod. He had to summon all his strength to speak. 'Yes—they will part the curtain of time to delve to what lies there at . . .'

Aelfric's head drooped. He leaned against the tree for

support. 'They have power—they believe that they . . . that they . . .'

'But it's not only that!' Uncle Alistair was insistent. 'It's you they want!' Uncle Alistair repeated in a low, urgent voice. 'They're after you! I can feel them pulling at your body! They want you! They believe you will help them, go over to them!'

'Yes!' Aelfric stared helplessly at the windows of the house. 'They are draining my strength! They are dragging me to . . . they are strong . . . *very*.' The warrior's voice faded, but defiantly he said, 'They shall not have me! I will resist! I must . . . oh, help me!'

Aelfric winced in acute pain. The chanting inside the Grange increased and he doubled in agony, but then stood up, still clutching at his stomach.

'They *are* strong!' Uncle Alistair whispered. He watched Aelfric writhe and claw at his chest. The full reality of Sir George's power seemed only to have struck him now.

'Oh!' Aelfric sank to the ground. He lay on the grass and began to shudder uncontrollably.

'What can we do? Oh, what can we do?' Maddy reached out to Aelfric. He grasped her hand weakly.

'I—I—they are pulling at my mind!' Aelfric forced out his words through chattering teeth.

The murmur inside the Grange increased in intensity.

'Help me!' Aelfric urged. 'I do not know if I can resist this pull much longer! Help me! Help me!'

13

Aelfric shuddered as the chanting from the Grange continued to swell. It spilled out of the house on to the lawn. Aelfric groaned, slumped on the grass, and began plucking at his face with his hands.

'Look over there!' Uncle Alistair whispered from under the invisible dark of the branches. The Grange windows were aflame with hundreds of candles, though the eerie light did not reach far across the shadowed lawn. Now those strange flames bunched and receded, bunched and receded, like a black pulse, like the beating of a sinister heart. It was as if the flames themselves had taken on the rhythms of the terrible chant within the house.

Inside, the assembled crowd bowed several times. They flung their arms into the air with a final, ear-splitting shout.

'The end of time!'

Maddy lifted her head. Aelfric's head had dropped forward. His face seemed shrunken and quite dead. Where was the light now? 'Help us! Help us!' she silently cried.

Her gaze swept up the lawn to the flickering light from the windows which spilled out over the terrace. For a moment the inside of the house spun out of focus. Sir George's guests became obscured from view, as though a black cloth had been drawn over them. Then they appeared again. Looking at this made Maddy dizzy. She could not make sense of what she was seeing. She watched, breathless. It happened again. The neat panes of glass of the French windows filled with cloudy black and the figures inside disappeared. That was when Maddy realized. She had seen that black before. It was the fathomless black of the suitcase.

Ralph felt uneasy. A tingling disturbed his fingers. Around him the lawn, the bushes, the beech tree and the house grew thin, transparent. Ralph had experienced this before. He started to feel giddy, as if everything was about to rush away. He felt the pull towards the end of time.

Uncle Alistair, however, was motionless under the beech tree. He scanned the flaring windows. Finally, he went over to where Aelfric was lying.

'Aelfric!' he whispered under the shelter of the branches. 'Aelfric! Wake up! Try! You have to! The Light! Remember the power of the Light!'

Aelfric swung his powerful fists in front of him as if he feared someone had come to attack him. But then his eyes opened and he saw Uncle Alistair's anxious face above him.

'Oh!' he gasped, 'it's you! I thought ... I was falling ... falling ...'

'You must hold on!' urged Uncle Alistair. 'Don't let go, whatever you do!' He took Aelfric's trembling arm and tried to help him up.

The deathly black shadow seeped once more across the windows of the Grange and Aelfric fell silent as stone. His mouth opened and shut and he tightened his grip on Uncle Alistair's arm.

'The end of time!' he muttered aghast. 'They have almost won through!'

The darkened rhododendron bushes drank Aelfric's dreadful words into their leaves.

'What?' Maddy turned her head quickly. She could barely make him out.

Aelfric stumbled in his speech. 'They are putting their

hands into... to come to the border of... the end of time... and it will...'

'The end of time!' Aelfric's words pierced Ralph's mind. There was something which had been bothering him for some time, something he had not said before. 'Is this really the end of time?' he asked. 'Wasn't that when you were supposed to wake up?'

Aelfric withdrew his arm from Uncle Alistair and sagged against the massive trunk of the beech tree. Ralph's words had moved him deeply. 'You are right, little one,' he said. 'It took a child to reveal the truth to me!'

'What do you mean?' Uncle Alistair's voice came sharp in the darkness.

'I should not be in the body now!' gasped Aelfric. 'My time has been and gone. I am out of place here. It was only at the end of time that I should awaken and then— somehow—I did not know—give an—account of myself. Now here I am on the brink of the end of time—for that is surely what lies within that dreadful place! I must go forward to meet it! Within that place lies my destiny!'

'No!' Uncle Alistair's denial sounded like a pistol shot. 'If you enter there—you will destroy yourself! They will take you! You will fall into their hands! You will...'

'... will I?' Aelfric's eyes closed in total exhaustion and his fingers clenched. 'But I am no longer what they think! I am not what they believe! I have passed beyond... I now know which way is the more powerful! I have taken the path of light and the Light calls us to lay down our lives if need be. This is the moment for which I awoke! If I can break what they are doing... I must try! I must!'

'I see...'—but it was clear to Ralph and Maddy that Uncle Alistair's assent did not come easily.

'There is nothing to regret! Not a word! This way is... is... the way forward! In the cave I have gained...

everything! It is a little deed, a tiny thing, to shine in the darkness—to offer myself—for it is all I have to offer now. This I must do! To turn away would be to turn from the truth—to return to darkness! But there is one thing I ask!'

'Name it,' said Uncle Alistair. 'Anything!'

'In the chamber ... were ... others who slept by me ... Perhaps they have also been kept for this day.

'Awaken them, if you can. Then I will enter with more gathered at my heels than dust! But give me the case, too! With that I shall confound them! The Aelfric they expect will not be the Aelfric who comes!'

'Go in the power of the Light!' Uncle Alistair urged. 'I will do what I can!'

Without another word, Aelfric began to walk towards the house. The dark light from the candles at all the windows enveloped him. He held the case tight. It was in his charge.

'We must go now!' breathed Uncle Alistair. 'If it was dangerous before, it is a hundred times more dangerous now! Quick! We have a task to perform!'

They thrashed back through the dense bushes, not caring what noise they made now, and hurriedly climbed the wall.

'What's Aelfric doing?' asked Maddy, once they were back on the path. 'Will he be all right?'

'It depends what you mean,' answered Uncle Alistair. 'I am afraid we won't see him again.'

'Oh!' Maddy suddenly realized the full meaning of Uncle Alistair's words. She looked back with great sadness to the Grange, feeling that something precious had been torn from her.

Aelfric opened the French windows and walked into the middle of Sir George's gathering. The guests were astonished. A gasp rippled round the room.

Aelfric's tall presence commanded silence. He stood his ground as they swung to face him.

'I am Aelfric!' he declared.

Confusion broke out among the guests as they questioned one another. Could this be true? Questions erupted into argument. Aelfric should not have appeared in such a manner! But the warrior's demeanour convinced them and they fell silent.

Sir George was behind a table set with black candles. 'Welcome!' he said. He lifted his palms in greeting. 'You may help us roll back the boundaries to ...'

'Silence!' ordered Aelfric.

Shadows swept round the room at this word. There were urgent whispers. The candle flames trembled. Sir George's face darkened. Something was wrong. Aelfric's appearance was not as he had planned.

Aelfric summoned his strength. 'This gathering is an abomination! You have resisted the call of the Light and chosen to cleave to darkness. And your mischief would unleash the powers of ruin and destruction! You are blind and wilful and greedy! This must cease!'

'Enough!' Sir George cried out in rage. 'How dare you defy me!'

He lifted his hand and a great, cloudy form of blackness hurtled at Aelfric. It caught him in the chest and he staggered back. The pain brought tears to the warrior's eyes and his forehead dripped with sweat.

'You may take me,' said Aelfric, panting, 'but no other will you have! I know what you have sought—a path to the end of time! There, you believe, is great power for the taking. But your blindness has led you only so far. Beyond the end of time lies the greatest treasure, for that is where the Light is to be found, but you have turned your backs on it!'

'Silence!' Sir George screeched.

Some of the guests shifted their feet. Something was wrong, though they were not sure what. There was a reservoir of strength in this battered warrior which threatened them all. They knew they dare not challenge him. They feared the living power in him.

'You wished to enter the cave of black stars and, through me, come to the end of time. Yet you lacked the means of entry, for it never came to you. Your fumbling will only bring judgment upon you! Fire will fall on your heads!' Aelfric held up the case. 'This is what you seek! I swear to you, what you have sought, you may have, though it will scatter you like chaff!'

'Stop him!' Sir George yelped in terror.

One or two men moved purposefully towards Aelfric, but most of the guests were too troubled or too confused to act.

Aelfric placed the suitcase on the floor and opened the lid. Instead of the darkness, an intense, pulsing light filled the bottom of the case. Aelfric lifted his arms.

'The truth is more than you know,' he said, 'and now is the time for truth! Behold, the Light!'

The light shifted and parted in the case. It rose through the sides in a great wave. It was the light of galaxies and supernovas. It glowed with the light of the beginning of creation. From the case rose strands of light, full of promise, and these strands twined into the shape of a spreading tree which shone and shimmered in the midst of Sir George's assembly.

From the depths of the case—out of the light—from beyond everything, from before everything, there came a song. That song was without words, sung without lips: no human ear could hear it. It was old, older than the earth. It was a song which went back to the beginning of time—and before—to the end of time—and beyond. It was a song

157

which summed up the new life of spring and the ripe fruit of autumn. It was a song which wound eternally through the earth for those who were tuned to it. Each person understood this song, because it was *their* song. The song had known them in the womb and called them into the world. It knew their deeds and thoughts, their waking and their sleeping, their past, their present and their future. It pierced them to the very centre of their being.

Sir George screamed and clapped his hands over his ears. The notes he heard caused him to shake his head in pain. He hated it. He could not bear it. He wanted it to stop!

Others were grasped by beauty, their hearts riven to the core. Some sensed a great shame sweep over them: they wanted to turn to the forgiving source of that song which called them once more to the welcoming arms of light. But only one of all those gathered there—the middle-aged man, his face lit with delight—walked to the rim of the case and knelt by its edge.

'No! No!' Sir George realized he had lost control. Nothing was going as he had planned. The prize was slipping from his fingers. With his hands still over his ears he pushed his way through the crowd... only to stop, amazed.

As he approached, the shimmering tree of light dissolved—and he was facing a flaming sword!

'This is the end of time for you,' said Aelfric to Sir George. 'From here there is no turning back!'

The light from the case grew stronger, fiercer. The black-flamed candles suddenly blazed with light, swallowing the darkness, enveloping Aelfric and the Grange.

The cloudy sky above Uncle Alistair, Ralph and Maddy pressed down with black fingers. An alertness like an electric current in the earth was running through the trees and under the soles of their feet.

'We must hurry!' said Uncle Alistair.

'Where are we going?' asked Ralph.

'To the schoolhouse!'

The schoolhouse lay across the road. Though they could see it, reaching it seemed hardly possible. A tide of solid air beat against them. A crushing weight pressed on their heads. They thought their lungs would cave in. Maddy felt as if some creature, like a dragon, had dug its way out of the earth to take flight above them. The creature hung ready to strike. Danger filled every corner of the night.

Uncle Alistair, Ralph and Maddy pulled, dragged themselves across the midnight road. There was no one about. It was late, and only a few, scattered lights were showing in the houses.

'Here!' Uncle Alistair panted and gulped for air. He struggled with the gate leading to the schoolhouse path. It swung open and he forced himself in with Maddy and Ralph heaving after him.

Then—the air was clear. There was lightness. Just a ringing in the head, circling behind the eyes, where all the weight had been concentrated before.

'Now!' ordered Uncle Alistair as he bounded up the path. Stopping by the dustbins, he rummaged in some earth-filled pots which stood by the door.

'Luckily for us,' he said, 'some traditional village habits survive. Here's the key!'

He fumbled with the lock. It turned with a decisive snap and the schoolhouse door creaked open to airy darkness.

'It's all right,' he said, 'I know where the lights are!' He began clicking switches on and off in the gloom. Lights sprang to life and dimmed till he found the one he wanted—the one over the picture of the horsemen.

'Now, let's see!'

They hurried into the hall and Uncle Alistair tore the sheet to one side. What they saw took their breath away. The horsemen were tilted at full gallop with their vizors down. Their horses were pelting, straining at the neck. Above them paint, black and glistening, like a storm cloud, was seeping in slow drops to engulf the figures beneath. On the left, the black stars, the stars within Aelfric's chamber, had massed to obscure the warrior's slab.

'You see, there is peril!' said Uncle Alistair. 'Great peril! We must call on the Light!'

Uncle Alistair gazed at the picture. His face was drained and paper-white in the strong artificial light. His lips moved soundlessly. He pleaded with such intensity that sweat glistened on his forehead.

Ralph absorbed his uncle's wordless appeal, but all he could think of was Aelfric. His last sight of Aelfric kept coming back. Again and again in his mind Ralph saw the warrior turn and walk up to the Grange. Aelfric had lost everything; he was utterly alone and out of time. Yet he had stepped into the midst of Sir George's assembly. But why? There was one word, only one word, which formed in his mind: sacrifice.

Sacrifice! That word thudded in Ralph's head like an earthquake, like a heartbeat, like an echo. Sacrifice! Aelfric had given himself to save them all from the destruction Sir George would unleash.

Uncle Alistair was touching the painting now. The fingers of both his hands flattened against it. He was straining and pushing. The figures shivered under his touch.

Maddy was very still. She sat with her back to a cold radiator. She was tired out.

'Please!' Ralph could make out the one word his uncle

was saying. 'Please!' That was what he was saying—
'Please!'

The villagers of Lower Chernton gossiped about that
night for months afterwards. What exactly had happened?
A freak wind, most said, though the meteorologists were
hard pressed to say where this wind had come from. Some
saw a scatter in their gardens, like leaves, and heard the
sounds of footsteps running. But they could not be sure.

The wind howled up the High Street, there was no
mistaking that. It shattered shop windows in its passing.
Out at Marlow's Farm, that mound with the ring of
trees—Aelfric's Hollow—was badly hit. A few of the
trees came down.

And then, well, some said they saw—but nobody was
very sure *what* they saw, or if they had seen anything. It
brushed by them, whatever it was. People in the village
had been seeing things, there was no doubt about it,
though that was the last night. The appearances stopped
after that.

There were some old folk who knew the story of Millie
Rawlings, the parlourmaid, and what she had encountered
on the road in 1873. They thought that the horsemen had
appeared again, but they only spoke to each other about
it. When you are very old or very young nobody is
inclined to believe you.

The earth trembled under Aelfric's Hollow. Uncle
Alistair sank to the schoolhouse floor and waited. The
trees swayed on the mound. The wind screamed up.

The gusts of wind hurtled the length of the village in a
terrifying shriek. The pub sign in the High Street swung
madly. The dustbins put out for the following morning's
collection bounced down the road and scattered their
contents.

Then it happened. A swell and a burst, as though forms were emerging from the tip of a wave. The horsemen rode out. They rode out into the darkness. The hooves of their horses screamed and whistled through the night air. The knights galloped across the fields with their lances thrust forward. Their armour glinted in the moonlight and sparks fell from their spurs. Foam dripped from the horses' mouths and their eyes were wide and rolling.

On they rode, the horsemen, out into the night. To pierce it with their lances. They hardly touched the ground. They had been summoned to combat the darkness. This was their call. For this they had endured the long centuries of sleep.

The wind reached the Grange and snatched at the chimney-pots. One rolled and smashed on the tiles of the roof. For a moment the house held its breath, timeless, sucked into itself.

Aelfric stood bathed in the glow from the case. Truly, he was a warrior of light. He heard the pounding of the hooves in the distance, the pounding of the horses in his head. He sensed the sky above him bend in a low, weighted curve to the earth. He lifted empty hands to Sir George's guests around him. He gave himself to what had bid him go forward.

Now there was nothing. Nothing. Only the end of time.

The end of time: that was when—such a shame, a historic house and a listed building, too—the windows of the Grange exploded in a sheet of flame. Glass smashed and flew in all directions. The paint on the frames blistered and peeled. The timbers of the ceilings blackened and burst into licking fire. The roof of the Grange heaved and sagged and caved in. Suffocating smoke surged through every floor and a falling, flaming shower of debris filled every part of the house.

There were screams and panic. Guests were choking and gasping and running, rushing out into the garden through the French windows. Some fainted, overcome by the heat and smoke, and were laid on the grass.

Uncle Alistair picked himself up from the floor.

'We're still here,' said Maddy timidly.

They had heard it pass over them; they had listened to the wind scream above the schoolhouse roof.

'We are indeed!' said Uncle Alistair.

'So...' but the remainder of Ralph's sentence was drowned by the deafening siren of a fire engine.

They hurried outside and saw blue flashing lights and a team of firemen dressed in yellow. They heard the crackling of two-way radios. The Grange was burning. The house was on fire. The sky filled with a dull, orange glow.

Uncle Alistair, Ralph and Maddy watched as flocks of dizzy sparks and plumes of thick smoke rose above the trees. Hoses lay across the road, drawing gallons of water from the mains. The wind died down all of a sudden.

'Goodness!' said Maddy.

'I suppose it is,' said Uncle Alistair with feeling. 'A rather severe kind of goodness, though nobody will recognize it as such. Still, we know what happened—and what almost happened. I doubt anyone else will.'

'What about all the people?' asked Ralph.

He had scarcely finished speaking when two ambulances screamed down the High Street and stopped behind the fire engines outside the Grange. Uniformed men hurried with stretchers, in through the gate to the garden. One or two figures emerged, unsteady on their feet. A couple were carried into the back of one of the ambulances. One woman appeared, coughing, with a blanket thrown over her shoulders. It was the woman with the long black hair.

The first spots of rain began to fall.

'Rain!' said Maddy in excitement. 'At last!'

Streams of water poured out of the sky to douse the fire. The rain came to break the blistering heat and drought of weeks and renew the earth. It was what the land needed. It was what the farmers wanted. To Ralph the rain seemed like a new beginning.

'We ought to go,' said Uncle Alistair. 'There is nothing for us here. The fire brigade and the ambulance men can sort everything out now. Aelfric . . .' but Uncle Alistair bit his lip and could not complete what he was going to say.

'I want to go,' said Maddy.

'Yes,' said Uncle Alistair, 'we ought to leave this to finish itself now. But we'll get soaked. At least,' he laughed, 'at least we'll be able to sleep tonight without the worry of anyone or anything trying to break in!'

14

Ralph woke with a start. He was in the attic room at Uncle Alistair's house. It was morning. He got out of bed, went to the window and looked out at the garden beneath him.

The lawn was jewelled with raindrops glittering in the sun. Grey clouds bobbed in the sky, but it was clearing. It would be another sunny day. The rain had broken the heat, though, and a grateful hush had settled over the woods and fields.

It was a morning like any other, but Ralph knew that something deep had happened in the village. Sir George and his guests had been defeated. The disturbance in time had been halted and the appearances would cease. But Ralph also knew that behind the obvious renewal the rain had brought, those 'seeings' had brought their own hidden renewal to the villagers. Lives had been altered and pasts had been mended. Today was not simply a continuation of yesterday. Ralph had changed, too. In recent days he had come to understand his Uncle Alistair a little better.

The garden wall was a wall again; stone was stone. Things were solid again. They would not yield and grow transparent any more. They were what they were.

When Ralph came downstairs, Maddy and Uncle Alistair were talking in the kitchen. The radio was on. A steaming kettle stood by the cooker and the smell of fried egg was in the air.

'Ah, Ralph!' greeted Uncle Alistair. 'I trust you slept well.'

'Uh!' replied Ralph, who was not at his best in the mornings.

Uncle Alistair helped himself to another slice of toast. 'You see, Maddy,' he was saying, 'going into that room was the worst thing Aelfric could imagine, but it was the thing he had to do—the only thing he could do. He knew that when Ralph mentioned the end of time. Suddenly, he realized the purpose of waking up. Sir George and his guests were expecting Aelfric to side with them, to part the curtain of time for them. But Aelfric had gone beyond that. He brought with him something Sir George and his cronies could hardly begin to understand—not what lay *at* the end of time, but what lay *beyond* it.'

'I think I see,' said Maddy, doubtfully.

'We ought to go out today.' Uncle Alistair stretched. The fresh, morning sunlight poured in through the kitchen window. 'I feel like sitting by the river. The grass is drying now.'

At that, the phone rang.

'Oh, bother!' Uncle Alistair frowned. 'I hope it's not your mother, Ralph. She wanted you to ring her.'

He went into the hall and picked up the receiver.

'Hello? Oh, hello, Nick!'

'Good morning! How are you today?'

Ralph and Maddy looked at each other. What had Nick found at the schoolhouse?

'Yes, we would,' said Uncle Alistair. 'We'll be right along.'

He listened for a while longer. 'The Grange—burned to the ground?' Uncle Alistair sounded shocked. 'Yes, we'll be along in a few minutes. We'll see you then.'

Uncle Alistair put down the phone and stuck his head

into the kitchen. 'Did you catch that? We're going to look at the picture!'

There was... there was definitely a different atmosphere on the road as they walked to the schoolhouse. Ralph felt it and so did Maddy. The air above them was clear—there was nothing weighing down on them now. Something had gone, though by looking at the trees and hedgerows you would not have been able to tell that there *had* been anything there.

They came to the schoolhouse gate. Across the road a dismal pall of smoke still hung over the ruined shell of the Grange. The windows had been knocked out, the roof had caved in, and the attractive stone was discoloured and blackened. The house was a complete ruin.

Ralph, Maddy and Uncle Alistair filed inside the schoolhouse. Nick Fleming was waiting for them.

'There you are!' he waved. 'Come and see!'

Now there was no sheet hanging over the painting.

'It seems to have settled somehow,' he said, tapping it with a forefinger.

'So it has,' agreed Uncle Alistair.

In the picture, the figures of the four horsemen had sunk back into the paint so that their previous liveliness had been lost. The horses were at rest, chewing grass with their heads down, while the horsemen were alert, perhaps for any possible attack which would call them to defence. In Aelfric's chamber a figure lay asleep on the slab and the black stars were painted evenly around it in medieval decoration. The painting was, truly, only a painting again. They could all see that. The knights had returned to their original substance.

'I don't know why,' said Nick, 'but anyway I reckon it's suitable for public display now. So many people are interested in coming to view it, and I don't think there's any reason to keep them away.'

'No, none at all.'

Uncle Alistair glanced down and saw Maddy frowning at the painting. She was obviously trying to work something out. It was on the tip of her tongue.

'But the Grange!' continued Nick, in a shocked voice.

'We saw it as we came in,' said Uncle Alistair.

'Quite an explosion! I can't think what they were up to in there. Vera Lyall put a few of them up at her Bed and Breakfast, but she wasn't keen on them. Funny lot! It's terribly sad—the Grange was such a beautiful house and I can't think what will become of it. And then there's Sir George, of course!'

'What about Sir George?'

'Haven't you heard? Goodness me! It's all over the village! Everyone was accounted for last night after the fire *except* Sir George! He seems to have vanished—gone! The firemen have trawled the wreckage of the house, but they haven't found a body. The others swear he was there, though. They say they were having a party and some candles started the fire. Anyway, Sir George is gone! Mrs Symmons thinks he was in debt and has done a bunk. Who knows?'

'Who knows, indeed?' agreed Uncle Alistair. 'We had better be going. I want to catch the best part of the day by the river.'

'Very wise! I might go out later myself.'

'And we'll give Sir George your regards if we see him!'

'You know,' said Uncle Alistair when they were outside again, 'the Grange *was* a beautiful house! I used to go there often to see Sir James. He was a grand old man. But,' he sighed, 'that's that! You were looking very thoughtful in there, Maddy.'

'It was only an idea,' said Maddy.

They ambled back to Uncle Alistair's house. A couple of cars passed them and they kept to the verge by the hedgerow.

'Well, Aelfric isn't *in* the cave of black stars any more. But somebody is painted there.'

'It's just a painting, Maddy.'

Maddy snorted. 'You know it isn't *just* a painting.'

'No, it wasn't. Maybe it is now. Paintings show us things and this one chose to show us something in quite a different way. But, tell me, who do you think could possibly be lying in the cave of black stars now?'

Ralph thought for a moment. 'Why, Sir George!' he said suddenly.

'Then I hope it does him a lot of good.' Uncle Alistair grinned. 'It's the best thing for him!'

Back at the house, they made sandwiches for a picnic. Uncle Alistair put some eggs on to boil.

'Hurry up!' insisted Ralph. 'I want to have a swim!'

'Yes, we ought to make the most of the day,' agreed Uncle Alistair. 'The radio says the weather's changing tomorrow. Rain from the west. Today's the last fine day.'

Outside, the river flowed on, slowing to the calm pool where bathers liked to swim in the summer. In the village, firemen trod through the splintered, charred timbers of the Grange, but even after an exhaustive search Sir George's body was never recovered. Some sightseers went to Aelfric's Hollow to look at the devastation of the gales. They recalled the legend which supposed there was a warrior asleep under their feet.

'I'll race you!' said Ralph, as they picked up their bathing things.

'I'll beat you!' said Maddy, and they rushed out of the front door.

Uncle Alistair walked into the living-room and watched them dash to the river. He had been left to carry the picnic bags.

He turned and tutted. On the mantelpiece, the carriage clock had stopped. Uncle Alistair picked the clock up and twisted its hands to the right time. With a flick of his fingers, he pushed a small lever and put the clock down again. Taking a deep breath of fresh air, he walked out of the house, across the lawn and down to the river, to join Maddy and Ralph. Ralph was already in the water and Maddy was hurrying to join him.

Inside, in the living-room, the carriage clock began to tick.

Also from Lion Publishing

A WITCH IN TIME

William Raeper

Ralph's uncle was different somehow from other people's uncles. For a start, there were those striking eyes—grey and green and deep as the deepest lake—that seemed to see right into you. As Ralph explained to Maddy, with Uncle Alistair in charge anything might happen. And right next door, just over the wall, was a mysterious new neighbour, Mrs Morgan, whose sinister figure cast no shadow—no shadow at all.

Dark magic is in the air in this spine-chilling story. As the mystery unfolds, events move rapidly towards the heart-stopping climax. Maddy, Ralph and his uncle stand alone and apparently defenceless against Mrs Morgan's terrible powers—yet always watching, guarding, is the grandfather clock, with its measured tick and timeless promise.

ISBN 0 7459 2073 X

MIDNIGHT BLUE

Pauline Fisk

Bonnie saw ropes hanging loose, poles falling away,
tree-tops sinking beneath her. As they rose, the sun rose
with them. Its warmth turned the dark skin of the fiery
balloon midnight blue. They flew straight up. Above
them, the sweet, clear music of the lonely pipe called to
them. Then the smooth sky puckered into cloth-of-blue
and drew aside. They passed straight through...

Winner of the Smarties Book Prize 1990

0 7459 1925 1

THE 'PANGUR BÁN' SERIES

Fay Sampson

Six beautiful, exciting adventures set in the dramatic era of Celtic Britain.

SHAPE-SHIFTER: THE NAMING OF PANGUR BÁN
ISBN 0 7459 1347 4

PANGUR BÁN, THE WHITE CAT
ISBN 0 85648 580 2

FINNGLAS OF THE HORSES
ISBN 0 85648 899 2

FINNGLAS AND THE STONES OF CHOOSING
ISBN 0 7459 1124 2

THE SERPENT OF SENARGAD
ISBN 0 7459 1520 5

THE WHITE HORSE IS RUNNING
ISBN 0 7459 1915 4

THE LITTLE WHITE HORSE

Elizabeth Goudge

'For a fleeting instant Maria thought she saw a little white horse with a flowing mane and tail, head raised, poised, halted in mid-flight, as though it had seen her and was glad.'

The beautiful valley of Moonacre is shadowed by the memory of the Moon Princess and the mysterious little white horse. To her surprise Maria Merryweather, a stranger to Moonacre Manor, finds herself involved with what happened to the Moon Princess so many years before. She is determined to restore peace and happiness to the whole of Moonacre Valley. And Maria usually gets her way...

Elizabeth Goudge's many novels have achieved great popularity with readers of all ages. Judged to be an outstanding book for children, *The Little White Horse* was awarded the Carnegie Medal in 1946.

ISBN 0 7459 1458 6

More stories from LION PUBLISHING for you to enjoy: